Cold Sinful Revenge

London Mafia Kings, Volume 3

Marissa Farrar

Published by Warwick House Press, 2022.

Chapter One
Jayden

On the flat roof of the high-rise building, the man yanked against the silver duct tape binding his wrists to the arms of the chair. A separate strip of tape covered his mouth. Blood trickled from one nostril, and the skin around his left eye had swollen with purple and blue bruising.

I walked a slow circle around the captive man.

"Do you know why you're in this position, Ronald?" I asked.

Because of the tape, he was unable to answer with words, and his eyes widened.

I patted him on the shoulder as though we were mates. "It's okay. You can nod or shake your head."

He shook his head, frantic.

Around us, the lights of London stretched in all directions. The night sky was free from stars—their illumination cancelled out by that of the city. It was two in the morning, but the capital was far from quiet. Sirens from passing emergency vehicles cut through the air, and somewhere, far below, a car alarm sounded.

I arched an eyebrow. "Really? Now why do I think that's bullshit?"

Two of my men stood back, their arms folded across their chests. They weren't there for their brain power. They used to be my father's men, but they worked for me now, Jayden

Wynter. I was the head of the Wynter Syndicate, and though I was fully aware that my youth went against me, I was determined to make up for it in ruthlessness and brutality, so ensuring no one else ever fucked with the Wynter family.

Not that there were many of us left. With my father gone, and my sister, Hallie, married into the Cornell family, it was basically just me.

But I had my father's legacy to uphold, and I wasn't going to disappoint him.

Ronald mumbled something against the tape.

I wasn't going to give him the chance to talk yet, but it would come.

"You're here because I got word that you were seen at the Dagenham warehouse in East London a few hours before a bomb went off that killed my father."

He shook his head again, but I didn't believe him.

Ronald was no innocent. He worked for the Gilligans, and I'd heard rumours of how he'd cut off a man's fingers a few weeks ago because the bloke had tried to push ahead of him at a bar.

I needed to know for sure. My gut told me that the Gilligans were responsible for murdering my father, but if I got proof, I wouldn't hesitate in destroying their family, just as they'd destroyed mine.

A cool breeze tugged invisible fingers through my hair as I walked another circle around Ronald.

I was trying to navigate a city that no longer had my father in it. I'd always had Marlon Wynter to protect me from the stresses of running a criminal syndicate, but now that buffer was gone, and so was the lifestyle.

The business was precarious, and so much of it was done on reputation. I was fully aware of what my reputation was like—a young Jack-the-lad who was more interested in fucking around and enjoying himself than running a multi-million-pound business.

I'd always felt sorry for Hallie for the weight of our father's responsibilities that landed on her shoulders. His expectations of her had always been far higher than they'd been of me, even though there was only a couple of years between us. Marlon Wynter had made no secret about the fact that he'd been reliving his youth through me. He'd encouraged my partying and screwing around, wanting me to enjoy myself. We'd both believed we'd had many years left before I'd need to even think about settling down or worrying about taking on the responsibilities of the business, and I regretted that now. I wish he'd armed me with the know-how I needed to reassure his business partners that I could handle things, just the same as Marlon Wynter ever did.

Uncertainty was a dangerous thing.

I reached to the corner of Ronald's mouth, flicked the edge of the tape to lift it from his skin, and then tore the whole thing off in one go.

Ronald screamed in pain.

I smirked. "You think that hurt? You're not going to last a minute. Now, answer my question, and tell me the fucking truth this time. Were you at the warehouse before the explosion?"

"No, I wasn't. I fucking swear it. Who told you that? Someone's talking shit about me, that's all."

I shrugged. "Oh, okay." I took a step closer. "I'll let you go then."

The stupid bastard's eyes lit up with hope. "Seriously?"

I flicked open the small but sharp knife I'd had cupped in my palm. "Of course not."

I stabbed the blade through the back of the man's hand, pinning his palm to the arm of the chair. He opened his mouth and howled.

"Now," I said, remaining dangerously calm. "I'll ask you again. Were you at the warehouse before the bomb went off?"

"No! I wasn't!"

I grabbed the handle of the knife and yanked it back out of his hand.

He let out a sob. His head hung heavy, chin to chest. Blood ran from the wound and dripped onto the flat roof.

Could I be wrong? People were known to lie to try and stir shit up. Who would benefit from me taking out the Gilligans? I knew one family—the Cornells—but they were there the night the bomb had happened. There was nothing preventing one of them from being killed, too, and it might have just been bad luck that my father had been the one to take the brunt of the blast. For all I knew, it could have been Tam Cornell who was the target.

I caught the back of the chair and dragged it across the solid tar and gravel of the flat roof. A lip of only a few inches curved up at the edge, but it was nowhere near enough to prevent someone falling off.

I faced the man towards the massive drop beyond, and, still holding the back of the chair, tilted it up so it balanced on the two front legs.

The man screamed. "No, no, please! Oh fuck. Oh fuck!"

"My hold is pretty fucking precarious here, Ronald. It's warm tonight, and my palms are sweaty. I'd hate for my fingers to slip."

I didn't like to see a grown man cry. Something about it made me uncomfortable, and I didn't like to be uncomfortable.

"Tell me what you were doing at the warehouse."

"I wasn't there. You've mistaken me for someone else."

"If you weren't there yourself, I'm sure you know someone who was. Give me a name, and I'll think about letting you go."

I gave the chair a little jolt, as though it was about to fall. He screamed and clung tighter to the arms, like that was somehow going to save him. I had no intention of tipping him over the edge. A man and chair in pieces on the pavement below would only attract attention.

When he died, it would be silent and invisible.

"I don't know anything, and the minute the Gilligans hear you're fucking over their men, they're going to come after you, too."

I tutted and shook my head. "Now, now, Ronald. Do you really think this is how you should be acting, considering your precarious position right now?"

"I'm a dead man anyway. If I tell you anything, and you let me go, the Gilligans will fucking kill me. If I don't say anything, then you will."

His words gave me reason to pause. "If they'll kill you, you must know something."

He realised his mistake.

"No! That's not what I meant."

"I guess the choice is that you can either tell me what you know now, or you can go through a fuck load of pain, and then tell me."

"Okay, okay. I made the delivery, but I didn't know it was a bomb. It was just a crate, and I was told where to leave it in the warehouse, that's all."

"Who gave you the crate? Was it one of the Gilligans?"

"No, a man called Doyle put things in place. There! I've given you a name. Get me the fuck away from here now!"

I had made a promise. Though I'd been having fun, I kept it and yanked the chair away from the edge of the flat roof. Ronald exhaled all the air from his lungs and slumped over, his relief at being on somewhat solid ground visible.

But I still wasn't done with him.

My voice grew harder. "How did this Doyle contact you? Does he work for the Gilligans?"

Ronald lifted his head. "I don't know."

He must be lying. "You expect me to believe you took orders off someone you don't even know?"

"If the price is right, yeah, I do."

I arched an eyebrow. "Someone paid you to set that bomb?"

"Like I said, I didn't know it was a bomb."

I gritted my teeth. This fucker.

"And how much was my father's life worth?" I growled.

He gulped, his Adam's apple bobbing. "Ten grand."

"Ten grand," I spat the words. "Is that all?"

He didn't seem to know what to say about that. That a man like Marlon Wynter had been taken out for the sake of ten grand would be laughable if it wasn't so fucking tragic.

I leaned down to speak in a low tone, ensuring he could hear me. "I'd have paid you ten times that if you'd come to me with that information and I'd have let you live."

Who was this man, Doyle? Was he linked to the Gilligans? By removing themselves from the order, were they protecting themselves? It didn't matter to me. Deep down, I knew they were responsible.

"What does Doyle look like?"

"I dunno. He was just a man. White, dark hair, about six foot. Nothing memorable."

"How did he contact you? Is his number on your phone?"

I'd already taken Ronald's mobile off him. I had people who could open it.

"I deleted everything," Ronald said. "You won't find any numbers or messages on there."

My father had a friend in the Met police. I didn't know how easy it was to recover things that were already deleted, but I was determined to try. If they were able to get the phone to digital forensics, I might be able to get the number of this mysterious Doyle.

I looked to the two men—Smith and Bateman. "I'm done here," I told them. "Finish things off."

They knew what was needed.

I turned and walked across the roof to where the lift and stairwell were built into a small extension.

Behind me, Ronald screamed for help, drumming his feet, bucking the chair backwards and forwards. If he wasn't careful, he'd knock himself off the roof. I wouldn't be able to put it down to being an accident. The police wouldn't class it as one with a knife wound in the back of his hand and his arms taped to the chair.

I caught the lift down to the ground floor, ignoring the shouts for help and the subsequent thuds of fists striking flesh.

I needed to drink, and I needed to fuck.

My blood scorched through my veins, and adrenaline pumped my heart. Maybe I should have finished things with Ronald myself instead of leaving it in the hands of my father's men—my men now.

But this was London, and there was always somewhere open. I'd be able to get a drink, and, looking how I did, it wouldn't be hard to catch the eye of some gorgeous, scantily clad girl who'd happily spread her legs for me. I glanced down at the white cuff of my shirt peeping from beneath my dark suit jacket. Droplets of blood marred the white material.

Fuck. I knew I should have worn black.

It wasn't so long ago that I wouldn't be seen dead in this kind of getup. I'd much rather have been dressed in a leather jacket and ripped jeans. But I was the head of the company now, and it was important I looked the part. The people we did business with wanted to deal with a man, not with someone who had the appearance of a thug

There was nothing I could do about the blood now. I'd have to wait until I got into a club and put some cold water on it—always cold on blood, never hot as it set it into the fabric. That was something I'd learned before I'd even become a man.

The thud of bass, music from the club ahead, reached my ears. It was the early hours of the morning, but still a queue for the place snaked out of the door and around the corner. Young women in towering heels and skirts that barely covered their pussies stood in small groups, giggling together, most already having had a skinful. Drunk girls didn't do it for me. I wanted a woman who'd participate in bed, not one who'd lie back, half asleep, while I ate her out. Maybe that would be some bloke's kink, but it wasn't mine. I wanted a woman to let me know exactly how much she loved my tongue inside her.

To my left, a cry of fright came from down an alley.

Feminine. Scared.

I should ignore it. I'd already dealt with enough trouble tonight. But something about the tone drew me in.

I took my knife from my pocket and flicked it open. Maybe a gun would be better, but even in London, gunshots caught people's attention, and the last thing I wanted was to attract the attention of the police. I had a couple of officers who were on my books, but there was never any guarantee that they could do what was needed to get the police off my back.

The cry came again, followed by the gruff tones of a man, and I stopped walking.

Fuck.

Almost every inch of me told me not to get involved, but that little part of me that wished I'd stayed to finish off Ronald also made me want to continue the fight. Strength burned through my muscles, and I wanted to put it to good use. If someone wanted to give me a reason, who was I to say no?

I followed the sounds down an alleyway beside the club. It was dark, the alley swathed in black, but I made out shapes and movement at the end. Figures stood between the large industrial bins that the staff from the club probably emptied the tons' worth of empty glass bottles into at the end of the night.

I was pleased I'd retrieved my flick knife from the back of Ronald's hand. It was still covered in his blood, but I wasn't worried about that.

The voices became more distinct now I was closer.

"—open those pretty legs for me, sweetheart."

A second voice. "You know you want to. Little whore. She's gagging for it."

There were definitely two of them, but I wasn't worried about that either.

The girl's tone was filled with fear, her voice trembling. "No, please. Just leave me alone."

"I bet her pussy is wet."

The tear of material ripping, followed by a shriek of horror from the girl.

"Fuck, look at those tits," one of the men growled.

If I was going to step in, I needed to do it now.

I moved quickly and quietly, flicking open the blade. Both men were fully focused on their prey and didn't notice me coming.

I grabbed the back of the t-shirt of the man closest to me and yanked him away, swinging him hard enough so he stumbled and slammed against the wall opposite. Surprise was my advantage when it came to there being two against one, but so was the fact that I wouldn't hesitate in killing these sons of bitches, where they'd probably run a mile from an actual fight and preferred to pick on defenceless women instead.

The other man spun towards me. "What the fuck?"

I didn't falter. I elbowed him in the face so his head snapped back, and, before he could regain his composure, I got behind him and caught him by the throat, wrapping my forearm around his neck. The first man had scrambled to his feet and was about to launch himself at me. A well-positioned knife point at his mate's eye put an end to that.

"I wouldn't, if I were you," I warned.

"Don't!" man number two squeaked.

The bravado I'd heard when they'd been taunting the woman had evaporated.

"Unless you want to see your friend's eyeball speared on the end of my knife, I suggest you both apologise to this woman and get the fuck out of here."

I hadn't paid any attention to the victim yet. All my focus had needed to be on the men so they didn't get one over on me. I didn't think she'd moved, though. She probably should have taken the moment and run, but perhaps she was worried they might chase her.

Man number one didn't even give me an argument. He left his friend in the dust and ran for the alleyway entrance—the same way I'd come only moments earlier.

I tightened my grip around the second man's throat, closing off his airway a fraction. "I suggest you do the same as your mate. I wouldn't want my knife to slip."

Giving him room to nod without the point spearing his eyeball out of his head, I withdrew the knife from his eye a fraction. As I'd expected, he nodded frantically.

I risked releasing him. There was the chance he'd not think straight and try to take me on again, but his friend was long gone and I was armed, so I had no doubt he'd lose. Luckily—for him—he made the right choice.

"Fucking cunt," he spat when he got far enough away. "I didn't want a little whore like that anyway."

I took a threatening step forwards, and he practically yelped in fear and then turned and ran.

"Prick," I muttered.

Pocketing the knife again, I pushed my hair back from my face. I didn't want to have to take on some traumatised girl, but I also wasn't going to just leave her there. She might have friends in the club who she could call on.

I stared down at the young woman huddled on the ground, and the realisation that I recognised her hit me with a shock.

Ivy fucking Gilligan.

What the hell was she doing here?

Chapter Two

Ivy

I gulped back a sob, my face wet with tears. I'd been so stupid, coming here alone. I'd thought it would be safe because there were so many people around, but I'd been wrong.

Things always went too far in my life. I was starting to think it was built into our genes.

Everything had happened so fast, and it was dark, so I hadn't realised who my rescuer was until the two men had gone and he turned to face me. The absolute last person I'd wanted to get involved was Jayden Wynter.

This arsehole had a reputation for being no better than the two men who'd tried to rape me.

I scooted back even farther, my back pressed to the dirty brick wall. The ground beneath me was filthy, too, and my dress had rucked up so the bare skin of my thighs and bottom scraped against the pavement. Was he going to finish off what they'd started? Could he even have been in on it, and this whole thing was a setup?

But no, from the way he'd handled those two, I didn't think they'd known each other. I'd genuinely thought one of them was going to end up with his eyeball quivering on the end of Jayden's knife at one point. I wouldn't have admitted it to anyone, but a part of me wanted for exactly that to happen.

I couldn't shake off the feel of those men's hands on my skin, like their fingerprints had left a physical mark on me. The scent of them—stale alcohol, cigarettes, and sweat—still filled my nostrils, and I could taste one of them in my mouth from where he'd grabbed my face and shoved his tongue between my lips. Nausea rolled through me in a slow, sickening wave, and I twisted to one side, sucking in deep lungfuls of air, praying it would pass.

It did.

I hated feeling this way—weak and vulnerable. Was this all I was without the protection of my family around me? Reduced to a nobody left bleeding in an alleyway?

A sense of shame filled me, and that shame was only increased tenfold because of the man who'd saved me. I didn't want help from a Wynter for anything, but it wasn't as though I could have been picky. If he hadn't come along, I didn't want to think about what would have happened.

Jayden stood over me, his feet planted on the ground. I didn't want to look at him, frightened to make eye contact, worried about what I might see in his eyes, or worse, what he might see in mine.

"You're hurt," he announced.

I lifted my hand and touched my temple. The contact stung. I remembered how the men had shoved me against the wall when they'd dragged me down here. The injury must have happened then. I wondered what other marks and bruises would reveal themselves over the next few hours or days. I pressed my thighs together, trying to expel the sensation of an unwelcome hand shoving between them.

Still, I didn't say anything.

He leaned in closer. "Do you know who they were?"

I shook my head.

"Didn't they know who *you* are?"

I found my voice. "No." The word barely made a sound in the night, and I cleared my throat and tried again. "They weren't from around here. I tried to tell them, but they didn't believe me."

"Shouldn't you have someone with you?" He glanced around, as though expecting people to appear. "Where are your brothers? Where are your father's men?"

I tugged down my skirt, doing my best to hide my legs. "They don't know I'm here."

"Why not?"

I remembered who I was and glared at him. "Because I don't need my father and brothers knowing everything about my business."

Aware I was still sitting huddled on the ground while he stood above me, I adjusted my position, planning to clamber back to my feet.

His gaze slipped down my body, and he raised an eyebrow. "Umm."

I glanced down, and my cheeks coloured. "Oh, shit."

The strap of my dress had torn, and the top had flapped down, revealing my left breast, right down to the areola. I snatched it back up, covering myself. "You don't have to look," I snapped.

"It was kind of hard not to. Nice tits, by the way."

"Fuck off."

He slid off his suit jacket and handed it to me. "Here. Cover yourself up."

A part of me wanted to refuse him, to say I didn't want anything from Jayden Wynter, but after what had just happened, I also didn't want to walk through the city with my dress so obviously torn. I slipped the jacket on over the top of my dress and buttoned it up at the front. It was far too big for me, but I was grateful for that. I remembered leaving my house, checking out my figure-hugging dress in the full-length mirror by the front door before I'd left to go out, admiring the way it had shown off my legs and accentuated my curves. Now all I wanted was to hide, and the jacket provided me with the opportunity to do exactly that.

Jayden put his hand out to me to help me up. Reluctantly, I slipped my smaller palm into his far larger one. His skin was warm and dry, and the pressure around my fingers felt good. He helped me to my feet.

I wobbled on my five-hundred-quid Louboutin heels.

"Can you call a driver?" he asked. "Get someone to pick you up."

My stomach sank. If I did that, I'd have to go home with a torn dress and bloodied face. While I no longer lived under my father's roof, I had live-in staff who were on his payroll and who would report back that I'd come home in the early hours of the morning in a state. Then my father and brothers would demand to know what had happened, and I didn't want to tell them.

He must have seen my hesitation. "You don't want to go home?"

"If I go back looking like this, questions will be asked."

"Okay," he said slowly. "Is there someone else you can call? A girlfriend you can go and stay with, perhaps?"

I didn't want anyone to know my secret, and I certainly didn't want Jayden Wynter to know. He was an enemy of my family, and if he held something over me, he'd hold it over them, too.

I glanced away, filled with shame. "No. I don't have anyone."

I did, but no one I could trust not to say anything to my father or brothers. That was the trouble with coming from a powerful family—they had the ability to either buy out or threaten anybody.

When I'd been only six years old and at a new school, I'd made a friend right away. I'd been so happy to have someone who really seemed to like me, but then, years later, she'd told me that she'd only been nice to me that day because her father had told her she had to be or she wouldn't be getting any treats or pocket money. Even though I'd only been a child, I remembered sharply the betrayal I'd felt at that knowledge, the sense of how I couldn't even trust the people who'd told me they were my friends. And as the years had gone on, my suspicion of others had only increased, as had my belief that no one would ever actually care for me simply for who *I* was and not because of my surname.

I loved my two brothers and my father, but their love came with expectations. They were hard, violent men—just like the one standing in front of me now. Their protectiveness no longer felt like protectiveness. It felt like ownership. I wanted to live my own life outside of the umbrella of being a Gilligan, but how could I?

I hugged his jacket closer and tried not to inhale the scent of his cologne.

I studied his face, the full lips, the dark eyelashes, the cheekbones. It was unfair that someone like Jayden Wynter could look like that. He was like a beautiful but poisonous flower, luring you in only to leave you with a rash and a stomachache. I found myself smiling at the thought.

"What's so funny?" he asked.

"Nothing. I was just thinking how men like you aren't good for a girl's health."

"Men like me? You mean the one who just stopped you getting gangbanged by those pricks."

I bit my lower lip. Would it have gone that far? Maybe. I shuddered at the thought.

"So, what am I supposed to do with you now?"

I sighed. "I don't know. I'll go and get a hotel room for the night."

"Won't your family wonder where you are?"

"They don't even know I'm out. They'll think I'm tucked up in bed like a good little girl."

"A good little girl," he repeated. His tongue flicked across his lower lip. "Right."

My skin prickled with goosebumps at his words, a strange rush I hadn't experienced before going through me. I sucked in a breath, a part of me wanting him to say that again.

Good little girl.

I shook the thought from my head. What the fuck was wrong with me? After what I'd just gone through, that was the last thing I should be thinking. Maybe it was a reaction to trauma. Everyone was different.

His eyes had darkened with hunger, and I pulled the jacket tighter around my body.

I glanced around for my bag. "Oh shit."

"What?"

"Those fuckers took my bag."

Lines appeared between his thick, dark eyebrows. "Are you sure? I didn't see them with anything."

"It's a little clutch bag. It only had my phone, keys, and my credit card. How can I get a hotel now?"

"I'll pay," he offered.

"Why would you do that?" I eyed him suspiciously. Everyone knew Jayden Wynter had no love for the Gilligans. Word on the street was that he blamed us for his father's death. Maybe we *were* the ones to blame. It wasn't as though my father or brothers would have confided in me.

"You know where I live, right?" he checked.

I did.

"Oh, right. You mean *your* hotel?"

"It seems stupid you sitting out on the street when I can help you. Come back to mine and get yourself cleaned up. My sister still has some of her stuff in her old room. She's taller than you, but I'm sure you can find something of hers to change into."

"Your sister, Hallie? Isn't she a Cornell now?"

His eyes hardened at my words, and a muscle in his jaw twitched. I noted the reaction with interest. Okay, so he wasn't a fan of his sister having married Tam Cornell. And there was me thinking they were all happy families now. Hadn't that been the whole point of the marriage—so the Cornells and Wynters became one, and so owned a bigger territory than we did? But Marlon Wynter had been at the forefront of that happening, and now he was dead.

Could the alliance be falling apart?

It made me wonder if that had been the reason my father would have wanted Marlon Wynter dead? That was assuming he was even the one responsible, but it sounded like something he would do.

Jayden grunted. "Yeah, and she's about to pop out another little Cornell."

"That'll be your niece or nephew," I said.

He grimaced. "Linked to the Cornells via blood. Lucky me."

I thought he was lucky to have a new baby in the family, but now wasn't the time to press that on him.

"I don't think I should be seen going to your hotel either," I said.

He sighed with irritation. "Well, what am I supposed to do with you then?"

"You don't have to do anything with me," I snapped. "I'm not your responsibility."

He frowned slightly. "Are you not? Then why does it feel that way?"

"Well, I'm not."

I was tempted to hand him back his jacket, but I couldn't—not with the torn strap. I also didn't want to go stomping off in the middle of London at this time in the morning all alone after what had just happened. Those two men might still be lurking somewhere nearby.

I didn't have my phone to request an Uber, or any money, or even my keys.

Shit. What was I supposed to do now?

He folded his arms over his chest. "Look. I'm not just going to leave you in the middle of London with a torn dress and no handbag or phone. I might be an arsehole, but I'm not that much of an arsehole. You're coming back to mine. I'll get you sorted out, and then we can figure out what to do with you."

"Don't I get a choice in the matter?"

"No. You don't have any choice."

The most frustrating thing was that he was right.

"Fine," I muttered.

A black cab with its light on headed towards us down the street. Jayden stepped out and raised one arm to flag it down. I caught sight of the tattoos scrawling down the back of his hand and knuckles. He was in a suit, but the tattoos betrayed him for who he really was.

A gangster.

The cab pulled over, and Jayden stepped out into the road to open the rear door. He gestured for me to climb inside. Like he'd said, I didn't exactly have much choice. I was self-conscious in his jacket and my heels.

The taxi driver glanced in the rearview mirror, and a frown marked his forehead. He must have seen the bloodied mark on my temple, but he didn't ask if I was all right. Was that because he didn't want to get involved, or did he know who Jayden Wynter was?

Exhaustion swept over me, and I closed my eyes for a moment. Then I thought of something.

"Can I use your phone? I need to put a stop to my card. Those arseholes could be drinking at my expense right now."

"Of course."

He handed it to me.

He had a picture of him and his sister as his lock screen. They were both younger—teenagers, I guessed—and he had his arm slung around Hallie's shoulders as they both grinned into the camera in a position that was classically a selfie. Something about the photo softened me towards him.

I was able to download my banking app, log in, and put a stop on the card, so at least that was one less thing to worry about.

After I'd deleted it again, I handed the phone back to him. "Thanks."

I was aware that we were leaving central London, which was considered neutral territory, and heading into the Wynter territory of East London. Sharp spikes of panic went through me. What was I doing? Was I making a huge mistake? The phrase 'out of the frying pan and into the fire' went through my head. It was no secret that Jayden had been asking questions about his father's death and that his main suspects were my family members. What if he tried to use me to get back at my father and brothers?

Maybe then they'd show they cared?

My chest tightened. I couldn't think that way. I wanted to be treated as an equal, but it wasn't often women were in such a male, testosterone-filled society. I saw how my brothers used women as playthings, picking them up in bars and tossing them away again once they'd got what they wanted. God forbid someone actually developed feelings.

Jayden might not think much of the Wynter-Cornell marriage, but I'd watched on with something like longing in my heart. Hallie and Tam clearly loved one another. It was possible for people who were once enemies to become so much more.

I didn't even know what I wanted from my life. Someone to love me for who I was and not because of what my surname was? Was that too much to ask?

The taxi stopped in front of the grand frontage of the five-star hotel in Shoreditch, and a doorman hurried forward to open the rear door of the black cab. Since I had no money, I allowed Jayden to pay. I would pay him back once I replaced my card—not that he needed the money. Just looking up at this hotel gave me an idea of the fortune he must be sitting on.

It was the early hours of the morning, so the place was quiet.

Self-conscious, especially in the expensive lobby, I kept my head down, my blonde hair falling over my face. I didn't want anyone to see me, and I really didn't want anyone to recognise me. Of course, I could explain my situation—that a Wynter was actually offering me help—but questions would still be asked, and one of them would be what I'd been doing in the centre of London, alone at two in the morning.

It was a question I didn't want to answer.

But perhaps it would be better if someone *did* know where I was. If Jayden decided he wanted to use me to get back at my family, it might be an idea for someone to know my location.

My stomach twisted. I had no idea if I was doing the right thing or not.

"This way," Jayden said, striding across the marble floors, towards a bank of lifts at the rear.

Everyone he passed bobbed their heads in a hello, or called greetings of "Goodnight, Mr Wynter," even though it was technically closer to morning now than night. A few of them shot me curious glances, but I assumed they knew better than to question their boss.

He used a special key to call the lift, and, when it arrived, we both stepped inside. I was too aware of the small space, of the mirrors on all sides reflecting our faces back at us. For the first time, I saw the result of the attack. My hair at my temple was pink with blood. My eye makeup had smudged into panda eyes, and there were dirty marks on both my legs. Jayden's jacket hung mid-thigh, dwarfing me, but at least it covered my torn dress.

Our eyes met in the mirror, and my breath caught. I dragged my gaze away again. I was frightened of what he was thinking. Was he really helping me out of the goodness of his heart? Did Jayden Wynter even have a heart?

The doors pinged open, and I emptied my lungs, grateful to be out of there.

We stepped into an open-plan penthouse. I took in the huge space, the sparse furniture, the hard floors. While beautiful, there was little comforting or inviting about the vastness of the space. How must it feel to live here all alone?

Did Jayden ever get lonely, or was he too busy having parties and inviting strings of girls back here to keep him entertained?

I hoped he didn't think I was going to be one of those girls.

"You can stay here as long as you need to," he said, tossing his keys and phone onto a hallway console.

I stared at Jayden Wynter's face. I'd known who he was most of my life, but I'd never had any reason to either want to know him or get to know him. Our families were sworn enemies. Sure, we'd crossed paths at various events or even in restaurants or clubs, but we'd always given each other a wide berth. I knew his reputation of being a womaniser who cared only for booze and money, and laughed off responsibility.

I wondered what he'd heard of me.

The good girl who always did what her family told her. Who was sheltered by her overprotective brothers. I'd gone to a private school, kept my head down, got decent results in my exams.

We were around the same age—he had maybe a year or two on me, though he seemed older. Was it because he was a man? Or was it because of the amount of responsibility he now had on his shoulders?

He seemed different now—as though the death of his father had aged him. He'd always clearly been attractive, with his dark hair and eyes, the generous lips, and square jaw—but he'd always seemed young and wild with it. Now his hair was cut shorter—though still was long enough to hold a wave—and his face seemed harder, the cheekbones more prominent, the muscle in his jaw standing out. There was a new kind of glint in his eye. Maybe it had always been there, I didn't know him well enough to be sure. The clothes were different, too. Gone were the ripped jeans and leather jacket, replaced by the sort of suit that was made to measure and cost thousands.

It was probably a mistake, allowing him to help me, but what choice did I have? I hated to think what might have happened if he hadn't come along when he had. Just the thought tightened my chest, and I struggled to catch my breath, adrenaline pumping through my system, my heart beating hard.

I could slip into my house once I'd cleaned myself up and got a change of clothes. But then I remembered that my bag had been taken and the keys to my house had been inside. Shit. How was I going to get in without anyone noticing that I'd been out in the first place? Because of my family's work, my house was locked down like Fort Knox. I wouldn't be able to get back in without a key or someone else letting me in. Then the questions would start, and I didn't want to answer them.

Jayden frowned at me. "What are you looking at?"

I hadn't realised I'd been staring, and I turned my head, my cheeks heating. "Sorry, nothing. Just zoned out there."

"Do I need to get you a doctor? You are hurt."

I shook my head. "No, it's fine. Just a few scrapes and bruises."

The thought of the attack sent ice into my veins. Yes, it was only a few scrapes and bruises, and those injuries would heal within a week, but the memory of the utter terror and panic of the knowledge of what those men planned to do to me would stay with me far longer. The helplessness had been terrible, too. I'd always thought myself untouchable because of who my family was, but the moment I'd stepped out of the umbrella of that protection, that had been what happened.

Had it been my fault? Had I been asking for it? I guessed that was what those men would say if they were questioned—that I'd been wearing a short skirt and no bra, and that I'd had a couple of drinks and had been on my own. Why else would I have been doing all those things if I hadn't been up for a good fuck?

If only they'd known...

A tear trickled down my cheek, and I twisted my face and used my shoulder to wipe it away.

I caught him watching me with a frown. "You're not okay."

"It's been a long night. I'll be fine."

I still wasn't even sure I could trust him, but what choice did I have? I wished I had someone I could rely on to help. It wasn't that I didn't have friends—I wasn't that lame—but did I have ones who I could trust to keep their mouths shut? Well, that was a whole different thing. When you belonged to a family known for beating or killing anyone who went against them, it was hard to find people who wouldn't fold the minute they were asked something.

"Why are you helping me?" I asked him.

The corner of his lips curled. "Because I'm a gentleman, of course, and when I see a woman in distress, I can't help but offer my assistance."

I snorted at that. "Jayden Wynter is a gentleman? Since when?"

He put his hand to his chest. "You crush me, Miss Gilligan. What are you implying?"

"That the Jayden I know has never been a gentleman in his life."

He shrugged. "Maybe I've changed." He walked over to an expensive-looking cabinet. "Do you want a drink? It might help with the shock.

I glanced down to where my hands trembled. I spread open my fingers and then clenched them into fists again. "Yeah, sure. Why not."

"Vodka?" he offered. "It's Russian and good."

"Honestly, it's all the same to me. I'm not fussy."

He gave me a look and then shrugged and poured a couple of fingers of vodka into two heavy crystal tumblers.

"I didn't think you would be like this," I admitted as he handed me the glass.

He tilted his head slightly, curious. "Like what?"

"Nice," I admitted. "Kind."

His eyes narrowed a fraction. "I'm not."

"You're being nice and kind to me. Unless there are ulterior motives, of course."

Maybe there were.

A frisson of discomfort went through me.

I raised the glass to my lips and downed the drink in one. Fire burned down my gullet, and I gasped, my eyes watering a little.

Jayden hadn't even sipped his yet, and he regarded me with amusement. "Another?"

I shook my head. That one had been for the shock, but I needed to keep my wits about me. I didn't want to end up in another situation like I had in the alley beside the club.

"Let's find you something else to wear," he said. "This way."

I set down my glass on the coffee table and got unsteadily to my feet. I was still in my heels, and, upon seeing me wobble, Jayden put out his hand to catch mine.

"Easy," he said, as though I was a spooked horse.

I stared at where his fingers met mine. His grip was firm but gentle. His hands warm, where my fingers were cold. I looked up, my lips parted slightly, to meet his gaze. The air seemed to still all around us. I couldn't even draw in a breath.

He let go of my hand as though I'd burned him and took a step away, clearing his throat.

A little part of me was disappointed. Womanising Jayden Wynter, yet he didn't seem to even want to touch me. I remembered how, in the alleyway, he'd glanced down at my exposed breast.

He was the son of my father's enemy.

No, that wasn't even right. My father's enemy was dead now, and Jayden had stepped into his place.

He *was* my father's enemy.

Chapter Three
Jayden

What the fuck was I doing?

Ivy Gilligan was no better than the rest of her fucking family, and here I was with her in my own private domain, giving her expensive vodka and letting her have the pick of my sister's clothes.

Just because I'd found her in a vulnerable situation didn't change who she was. That she was small and curvy, and when she'd accidentally flashed her tit at me it had taken all my self-control not to cover her nipple with my mouth, didn't change anything either.

I should take her to a different hotel. Fuck. I should just drop her outside her father's house. It wasn't as though I didn't know where they lived. Why should I care if it meant she'd have a rough time of it?

I remembered what Leo Cornell had done to get revenge on the man who'd murdered Leo's fiancée. He'd taken the daughter instead. Was that what was going on in the back of my mind?

No. I had to be smarter than that.

It would be easy enough for the Gilligans to get Ivy back. They'd just send over their men, or even the police, to say she'd been kidnapped. I couldn't take her to another country, like Leo had done with Kaja.

I had a business to run.

I led Ivy down the hallway to the room at the end that had once been occupied by my sister before she'd been handed over to Tam Cornell like a prized cow.

I'd loved and admired my father, but even I had to admit that using Hallie as a way of securing our business was a fucked-up thing to do. It had been different when it had been Harvey Cornell who she'd been marrying—even if he had been a bit of a player and everyone knew it—but I hadn't expected for our father to then hand Hallie over to Tam after Harvey had been murdered on their wedding day. Tam thought too highly of himself—in my opinion, he still did—but even I had to admit he treated Hallie well now. Plus, they had a baby arriving any day.

I crossed the room to Hallie's walk-in wardrobe. It led through to an en suite bathroom.

"Here," I said, opening the door to reveal the walls on either side still lined with hangers, and storage boxes containing shoes and bags. Hallie had only taken her favourites with her. I think, when she'd first moved, she'd been conscious of the fact she'd been moving into Tam's space and hadn't wanted to take up too much of it herself. "Take whatever you want. Hallie won't miss it. The bathroom is through there, too, if you want to get cleaned up."

She stared at the floor. "Thanks."

I realised I needed to leave her alone if she was going to get changed. The memory of how her plump tit had hung out of the front of her torn dress flashed into my mind, and heat gathered in my cock. I could happily have stood there and watched as she stripped off my jacket and then that dress. I already knew she wasn't wearing a bra and I highly doubted her panties were much more than a piece of string either. My mouth watered, and I imagined cupping her tit in one hand, squeezing and massaging, while I covered her nipple with my mouth. It would harden and peak as I sucked and flicked it with my tongue.

"Jayden?" she said, raising her eyebrows at the door behind me.

Shit, I'd just been standing there, staring at her. She really was a pretty little thing—even more so with her makeup smudged and her dress torn. It seemed a shame to make her presentable.

I didn't want her to notice the bulge forming in my trousers—the lighter material of the suit was less forgiving than the more restrictive fabric of say a pair of jeans—and I turned to leave her.

I hadn't forgotten about the information I'd gathered from the man on the roof. I was going to need to do some digging if I was going to find out who Doyle was. My gut told me he worked for the same family Ivy belonged to. Once she'd sorted herself out, I'd use this opportunity to question her. Of course, she might cover for whoever he was. It was certainly possible. I couldn't allow my mind to be clouded just because she was pretty and vulnerable right now. Ivy Gilligan's allegiance was always going to be with her family, just as mine would be.

Not that I had much of a family left.

I found my phone where I'd put it on the side and did my best to distract myself by sending the name to some contacts to see if anyone recognised it. I didn't like to think there was a chance this man didn't exist and Ronald had been lying to me in the hope I'd let him go once he'd opened his mouth. That would put me back to the beginning.

I glanced at the closed bedroom door. Maybe not quite the beginning. Even if Ivy didn't know anything, she was close to the men who most likely knew exactly who had ordered the bomb set in the warehouse—her father and brothers, Greyson Gilligan, and Aiden and Bruno.

Doing my best to put the thought of Ivy Gilligan stripping off her clothes out of my head, I put my back to the door and focused on the rest of the penthouse. Even though my father had left this place to me, it still didn't feel like my own. I'd had to step into his shoes with regards to the business, but it was as though I'd stepped into his life as well. I felt like a boy trying on one of his father's suits only to discover it didn't fit me at all.

I didn't want to analyse that image too deeply. This was my life now, and I had to get on with it. I'd been forced to grow up, literally overnight, and maybe it would simply take me a little time for that suit to fit me.

The sound of water running came from behind the door.

Had she wanted to scrub off the remains of her assault? Because that's what it had been. Those two fuckers had assaulted her. I wished I could find them again and actually gouge out that arsehole's eye this time.

The open-plan living room and kitchen felt empty and sparse again without her in it. I enjoyed having another warm, breathing body in here. No, it wasn't even just that. I often had people here—men who'd worked for my father, or even Hallie came around occasionally to visit, though her husband tended to give me a wider berth. I'd never have said it out loud, but it was weird being here alone. I was a grown man and had no issues with being alone, but sometimes I caught the shape of my father moving through the room out of the corner of my eye and I spun towards it, expecting to find him—a part of me, just for one second, forgetting he was dead. It fucking freaked me out. Though again, I'd never tell a soul that a part of me was worried about ghosts.

I liked knowing there was another beating heart in the place, and that the heart had a sexy little body surrounding it was even better.

She emerged from the bedroom in jeans that clung to her thighs and backside—but that were a bit too long—and a t-shirt that stretched across her breasts. Now she'd taken off her heels, it was clear she wasn't much over five feet tall. She'd washed her face, so the makeup was no longer smudged under her eyes, and from the way her blonde waves were wet at the front, it looked as though she'd tried to wash the blood out of her hair, too. She hadn't done a very good job, though, and the attempt to wash it had only prevented whatever clotting had already happened, so the wound had reopened.

"You're still bleeding," I pointed out.

She brought her hand to her head. "Oh."

She pulled her fingers back and stared at the bloodied tips. Her skin paled, and I hoped she wasn't going to pass out.

"Come here," I instructed. "Sit. Let me patch you up."

"What are you going to do?"

"Just stop the bleeding. I'll be gentle."

She nodded and crossed the floor to perch on the arm of the sofa.

My stomach flipped that she seemed to trust me so much. After what she'd just been through, I couldn't help thinking that maybe she shouldn't. She knew who I was and what sort of things I was capable of. Why wasn't she more fearful of me? Was it simply because she was used to dealing with worse kinds of men at home?

I left her for a moment to retrieve the well-stocked first-aid kit I kept in the bathroom. Though my family had a doctor on its books, I still preferred to deal with things myself if I could. Answering other people's questions wasn't something I liked to do. Even though the doctor knew to keep his mouth shut, he was more for things like bullet or knife wounds than scrapes to the head.

I returned to Ivy with the items I needed. Some rubbing alcohol, a couple of plasters, and cotton wool pads. It wasn't exactly fancy, but it would do the job. She sat there with her hands primly linked in her lap, watching me carefully.

"Do you want another shot of that vodka?" I asked her.

She cocked an eyebrow. "You're not planning to stitch me up, are you? It's only a small cut."

I surprised myself by laughing. "No needles involved, promise."

I tipped some of the rubbing alcohol onto the cotton wool and then used it to dab away at the wound on her forehead. It didn't look too bad—definitely didn't need stitches—but the position it was in, with her hairline meeting the injury, made it harder to clean.

Ivy sucked air in over her teeth.

"You're doing great," I told her. "Just a little more. You can take it."

She lifted her gaze to mine, her blue eyes widening a fraction. Her lips parted, and a tension that hadn't been there only seconds before I'd opened my mouth appeared between us. An invisible magnet suddenly drew me to her, and I had the urge to claim her pretty mouth, to nip and suck at her lips, and drag her body hard against mine.

What had been the reason for her reaction? Had she liked it when I'd praised her?

I was tempted to say something else, but I couldn't complicate things like that, could I? I needed to stay focused, and trying to fuck my enemy's daughter was only going to muddy the waters. Besides, after what she'd been through that evening, I highly doubted she'd want another man pawing over her.

Doing my best not to meet her eye, I finished up and laid a plaster across the cut in a strip so it would catch the worst of the blood.

"There," I told her. "All done."

She gave a small smile. "Thanks."

"You know, you shouldn't go out without either friends or your father's men as protection."

She set her lips in a line. "Why? You were out on your own. You didn't need any protection."

"You know why. I only came to help because I heard you cry out. What if those men had spiked your drink so you weren't able to shout and I'd found you unconscious in the alley after they'd done what they wanted?"

"So I'm not supposed to go out in case someone spikes me? How about men just don't spike women instead?"

There was real anger in her tone, a fire to her. I guessed I should have expected that—she'd grown up in the Gilligan household after all. I reminded myself that they were my enemy. The ones responsible for my father's death.

"I'm not saying I disagree with you, but we both know that's not the world we live in."

"A fucked-up world," she muttered.

I wasn't going to disagree with her there.

"Can I ask you something?" I said.

She gave a one-shouldered shrug.

"Did your family set off the bomb that killed my father?"

"I don't have anything to do with things like that."

I pointed a finger. "That wasn't a no."

"How can I give you a yes or no answer when I don't know myself? My father doesn't want me to be involved in the business, not at ground level anyway. He has my brothers for that. He's pushing me to go into law or politics, something that might help things higher up."

"Is that what you want to do?"

"I don't know what I want to do. I haven't really been given the chance to work things out for myself yet. We don't talk about feelings in our family. Too much testosterone. You're expected to stay quiet and deal with things with your fists or a knife or maybe even a gun. No one wants to hear a woman whining, as my father would say. Wasn't it the same in your house?"

"Maybe, though I had—have—Hallie, and she always wanted to talk."

"But no mother."

"I guess that's why Hallie and I were always close. She kind of covered that role for me, even though she's only two years older."

"If you think my family killed your father, why aren't you using this opportunity to take revenge on them? I'm at your mercy. You could do anything you wanted to me right now."

"Maybe I believe in catching more flies with honey than vinegar." I thought of something else. "Do you know the name Doyle?"

She twisted her lips, considering it, but then shook her head. "Should I?"

"It was mentioned tonight in connection with the bomb that went off at the Dagenham warehouse. I thought you might know it."

"Sorry."

I sighed, my shoulders slumping. "How am I going to make sure you get home safely?"

She bit her lower lip, and I found myself transfixed at the tiny indentation her teeth made. "I'm not sure. At least I look respectable now."

"Is anyone going to question where you got your clothes?"

She gave a small laugh. "Would you notice if your sister was wearing something different?"

She had a point. "No, I wouldn't."

"My father and brothers have no clue. I could go home wearing a sack and they probably wouldn't notice. I'll say I left early to study at the library and someone stole my bag. I'll say they grabbed it from my arm and pulled me down at the same time, and that's how I got the marks."

"Your father won't be happy. He'll want to do something about it."

"I know. I'll have to figure out an area that doesn't have any CCTV so he won't be able to work out that I'm lying."

"He'll want a description."

"I'll say it happened too fast, that they came at me from behind, and pushed me to the ground, so I didn't see anything except feet running away. There won't be much he can do about that. He'll be fucking fuming, but that's all, and I expect he'll lock me away for weeks to come, claiming that he's protecting me."

Seemed she had it all worked out.

I frowned. "He won't actually lock you away, will he?"

"No, but he might as well. I had to take the tracker off my phone to slip out last night, but normally it's always on there. He knows exactly where I am and what I'm doing."

"He doesn't know right now."

A small smile touched her lips. "No, I guess he doesn't."

"So maybe you just shouldn't go back to him." I threw out the cheeky suggestion.

"And what, stay here with you? Wouldn't that be handy for you? A way of pissing off my family that fell right into your lap."

"You haven't fallen into my lap, as far as I can tell."

"You know what I mean."

She let out a sigh. "You've been kind to me, Jay, and I appreciate that. I don't want to bring the kind of trouble into your life that would hit you if I was to stay here."

"Maybe I welcome that trouble."

She shook her head. "That wouldn't be good for either of our families."

Despite myself, a spurt of anger and adrenaline went through me. Did she think I wouldn't be able to take on her father and brothers? Didn't she realise that was my whole focus right now—to push her family out of this city for good?

She'd been looking at me as she would a friend, but I wasn't that at all.

Chapter Four

Ivy

I was lucky that I lived within walking distance of the London Metropolitan University where I was studying. I got Jayden to drop me off at the university grounds on Holloway Road. The library would be open by now, so I'd go and read for a couple of hours and then make my way home and play out the whole 'lost bag' scenario.

Though I was now respectfully dressed in jeans and a T-shirt, I seemed unable to shake the sense of self-consciousness that had fallen over me. Maybe it was vulnerability, too. I'd never thought I'd be someone to be attacked in such a way, and, now I no longer had Jayden Wynter by my side, I felt more vulnerable than ever. I highly doubted I was going to run into either of those men here, and I'd been coming to this university for the past two years without ever feeling like I was in any danger, but I still couldn't shake it.

Jayden had surprised me. Of all the people to come to my rescue I'd have probably chosen him last, but now I'd spent time in his company, I strangely wanted to be back in it again. But it wasn't as though I could expect him to be my own personal bodyguard. He hated my family. He thought my father and brothers were responsible for the death of *his* father, and the truth was that they most likely were.

What would he do when he had his proof? Would he come for us? Would he enlist the help of the Cornells, as well? The thought made me fearful. Despite my father and brothers being overprotective and occasionally overbearing, I didn't want them to come to any harm. If they had to take on both the Cornells, and what was left of the Wynter family, they would be outnumbered. I didn't want anyone to die. Before last night, I'd have said I didn't want any of my family to die, but to my surprise, I discovered I didn't want anything to happen to Jayden either.

He wouldn't rest, though, wouldn't stop. I'd grown up with men like him, and vengeance wasn't something they simply let go.

An arm looped around my shoulder, and I jumped and lurched away. "Jesus."

The young man who'd put his arm around me raised both hands in defence. "What's got you so nervous this morning?"

"You just scared the shit out of me, Kyle," I snapped.

"Sorry, I was only trying to say hello."

A rush of irritation heated me from the inside. "You couldn't have just used words like a normal person."

He shrugged. "What are you doing in so early anyway."

"I needed some books from the library."

"You haven't got any of your stuff with you."

I'd normally have a laptop permanently attached to me, and I was conscious that I didn't even have my phone.

"I wasn't planning on staying long." I narrowed my eyes. "What is it to you anyway?"

"No reason. Just making conversation."

I prayed he wasn't going to notice how tired I looked or that I most likely still stank of stale alcohol and the bar and possibly even the alleyway, though I'd done my best to get cleaned up in the bathroom at Jayden's place. I wore my hair loose, so it covered the plaster that Jayden had used to stop my head bleeding. I liked to think I was normally well put together, and right now, I definitely wasn't. I'd used what products I'd found in Hallie Wynter's old bathroom, trying to freshen myself up, but it wasn't the same as having my own stuff. I'd considered using the en suite shower there, but I hadn't been able to bring myself to strip completely naked in Jayden's penthouse.

Kyle didn't seem to recognise any of these differences about me, however.

"You want some company in the library?" he asked.

Kyle and I were just friends, but he made no secret about the fact he wished it could be more. He'd asked me out on a couple of occasions, and he even tried to kiss me once at the student union on a night out with everyone, but I'd managed to duck out of his way. The whole thing had been kind of awkward and embarrassing, but he didn't seem to have got the hint yet.

"No, thanks. I'm not going to be long."

He shrugged and fell back a little, allowing me to walk on. "You've got my number if you change your mind."

That wasn't going to happen.

I lifted my hand in a half wave and put my head down and kept going.

The library was quiet at this time in the morning. I didn't have my student card that allowed me to buzz through the turnstiles, but the campus security guard knew who I was and let me through.

I loved this place. It was my favourite spot in the whole university. While the other students in my year hung out at the student union or in one of the numerous cafés, I preferred the solitude of the library. I wasn't someone who made friends easily, and big crowds made me nervous. I always felt like I was sitting on the outskirts of everyone else's conversations, embarrassed and awkward in case people noticed no one was talking to me. Then someone like Kyle did try to talk to me, and I brushed them off. I expected people thought I was stuck-up and arrogant, because I had money and a powerful family. Maybe people didn't make an effort with me because they were nervous about the repercussions?

Either way, it was just easier to hang out on my own. Books never judged, and I didn't have to second-guess them either.

I found a quiet spot in the corner and settled down to read with a book I'd selected off a shelf. I would be able to pass a couple of hours this way until it got to a reasonable time for me to make my way home again. If anyone had noticed me missing at home, I'd be able to give an explanation. Now the campus security guard had seen me here—as had Kyle—I also had witnesses.

I missed not having my phone with me. I wondered if the person I'd been supposed to be meeting last night would have tried to get hold of me. They clearly had cold feet, but they couldn't expect this to just go away.

When enough time had passed, I made my way home. I'd switched the expensive high heels for a pair of trainers back at Jayden's penthouse, so at least I wasn't having to walk in stupid shoes. I bit my lower lip thinking about those heels. Would I ever get them back? Maybe they could be an excuse for me to go and call on Jayden again.

I shook the thought from my head. No, I wasn't going to see him again. What had happened last night was nothing, it had just been a case of him being at the right place at the right time. And anyway, literally nothing had happened. Unlike his reputation, Jayden had been a complete gentleman. He'd not laid a finger on me. Was I disappointed about that?

The walk home took me twenty minutes. I hadn't slept all night and I was exhausted. All I wanted was to climb into bed and sleep—though I needed a hot shower first—but I braced myself for the onslaught of an interrogation about where I'd been all night.

Since I'd lost my key, I had no choice but to ring the bell.

I was relieved when it was my maid rather than one of my father's men who answered the door. Though this house was technically mine in name, it was run by my father's company, and it was his people who took care of the place.

"Hello, Mara," I said, stepping past the older woman. "I lost my key."

She frowned but nodded. "I can arrange to have another one cut."

"Thanks. I'd appreciate that." I paused then said, "And can you not mention it to my father. You know what he's like. He'd probably insist on having all the locks changed."

Mara gave me a knowing smile. "I won't mention anything."

I was going to have to tell my father I'd changed my phone, unless I was able to contact the phone company and try to keep the same number. What reason could I give? I had enough money that I didn't need to go to him, cap in hand, and ask for a new one. I had a spare credit card, kept for emergencies, in my room, so I'd use that. If he noticed the change, I'd tell him I dropped it and the screen smashed too badly for it to be repaired. I needed to cancel the contract with the old one, too, but I couldn't face it right now. I hadn't slept all night, and I was still shaken from the attack.

My plan had worked, and I should be pleased. There was the possibility I'd still have to tell him the story about someone stealing my bag if he noticed I had a new phone or he spotted a new bank card arriving, but so far, it looked like I was in the clear.

I shut myself in my bedroom and took a shower, scrubbing away any remnants of my disastrous night. The thought of those men's hands on me kept trying to penetrate my head, so I deliberately turned towards thoughts of Jayden instead.

I'd been raised on stories of how terrible the Wynter family were. My whole life, I'd been warned they were vain and weak and only cared about money. I was told they treated the people on their territory with contempt and failed to protect them.

When the Wynters joined with the Cornells through Tam and Hallie's marriage, it was all doom and gloom. All I heard was how the city would go to ruin now, how businesses would be driven into the ground, and how violence would only increase.

From what I could see, the only violence had originated at my family's hands, if what Jayden said was true about my family being responsible for the bomb that had killed his father.

I hadn't let him know earlier, but I had my doubts about that.

I wanted to see him again.

It was so stupid of me. What would be the point? The two of us could never amount to anything. God, there *was* no two of us. I'd spent barely a night in his company, and he hadn't so much as kissed me. Nothing had happened between us. The sparks I'd felt when he'd put his hand on mine and the deep-down shiver I'd experienced when he'd told me I was a good girl meant nothing. They were just stupid little reactions—something I probably wouldn't have even thought about if I hadn't already been traumatised from the attack.

I'd been told Jayden Wynter was cruel and thoughtless and impulsive, but the man I'd met had been none of those things.

It made me wonder what else my family had been lying about.

Why did my heart do that strange jolt when I thought of him? The tattoos, the dark hair, the intense eyes. The way he was living alone in that vast, empty apartment. I felt like there were always people at my home, how it was almost never empty, even if they were people I'd never asked to be here. How could he not be lonely? Grieving his dead father, too.

Was his sister around? Or was she too busy with her own life—her new husband and imminent baby—to worry about her brother?

I had the crazy idea I could talk to her but immediately pushed it from my mind. That would be overstepping so many boundaries, I'd have practically frog-jumped them.

Besides, I could just imagine Hallie Wynter's—or was it Cornell's now?—face if I showed up at Tam Cornell's house.

I would be asking for trouble.
And I was in enough of that already.

Chapter Five
Jayden

I caught a few hours' sleep to make up for my lack of it the previous night.

Fuck.

I couldn't get Ivy Gilligan out of my head.

The way she'd shivered when I'd told her she was a good girl.

I needed to shake those thoughts from my mind, but I found myself in Hallie's bedroom, observing the spot where Ivy had stripped naked only a matter of hours ago.

Why hadn't I just taken her? If it had been any other girl, I would have. In fact, I remembered having the distinct thought after leaving Ronald on that rooftop that I wanted to drink and I wanted to fuck. Instead, I'd ended up treating this girl with kid gloves, like I thought she might break if I so much as breathed on her in the wrong way.

What had Ivy Gilligan been doing down an alleyway in central London at two a.m.?

Had she really just been out for a bit of fun? If so, she'd failed drastically. She just didn't seem the type.

Her torn dress was still in the wastepaper basket in my sister's room.

I stared down at it, battling with myself not to fish it out again, and lost. I stooped down and plucked it out. The torn strap hung down, and the memory of her perfect breast hanging out of the front of the dress, exposed for all to see, flashed into my head.

What would she have done if I'd ducked my head and latched my mouth on to her nipple and sucked it, hard? I imagined her trying to push me off, while I only sucked harder, wearing her down until she eventually folded against me and gave in.

Blood rushed to my cock, filling and swelling my length. I brought her dress to my nose and inhaled deeply. I didn't think she'd been wearing any perfume, and yet I could still smell her on the cloth. Fuck. I was getting harder. Was she ever likely to ask for the dress back? I highly doubted it. Not only was it torn and would probably remind her of what had happened last night, but she didn't have any way of getting in touch, other than coming directly here. She'd lost her phone—or more accurately, it had been stolen—and so it wasn't as though we'd switched numbers.

I needed to focus on the name I'd been given last night, to pass it around and see if anyone else recognised it, but I couldn't seem to tear my thoughts away from the girl who'd been in my penthouse. Though she'd only been here for a matter of hours, her presence had permeated the whole place, her scent in the air, so now she was no longer here, it felt even emptier than before.

I held her dress at my nose once more and breathed her in. I pictured the spot that would have been right above her pussy. Could I pick up on the musky tang of her? I wished she'd left her knickers in the rubbish. I'd have kept them under my pillow and pulled them out whenever I wanted to get off.

My cock was painfully hard now, and I knew I wouldn't be able to do anything else until I'd dealt with my erection. I slipped my hand down the front of my sweatpants and curled my fingers around the hot, hard length. I edged my hips forwards, my cock pushing through the tunnel of my hand.

I swiped my thumb over my slit, rubbing the slick moisture across the smooth head, enjoying the sensation.

Needing more space, I edged my sweatpants and boxers down my hips, freeing my cock. I wrapped the silky material of Ivy's dress around the head, liking that I was getting my precum on it. I toyed with the idea of sending it back to her, of letting her know what I'd done. What would her reaction be? Disgust, I was sure, maybe mixed with a bit of shame? But I didn't care about that because it would also make her think of me. She'd picture my hand around my erection and be fully aware I'd been thinking of her while I'd been masturbating.

I released myself for long enough to spit in my palm and then grabbed my dick again, giving myself a satisfying squeeze. I nudged the head against the silky material, picturing it as Ivy's cunt. What would her pussy be like? How experienced was she? Would she be fully shaved or waxed? Would she be as tight as I liked to imagine? I'd love to have those curvy thighs around my face while I covered her pussy with my mouth and plunged my tongue inside her.

I'd seen the flicker across her face when I'd told her how well she was doing when I'd been cleaning her up. She'd liked it. I wondered how often she was praised for something she did, growing up in that household? Did the Gilligans have high expectations of their only daughter? Was nothing she ever did good enough?

I worked my dick harder and faster, my arse muscles clenched, my thighs taut. In my other hand, I clutched her dirty, torn dress, thrusting into it as though it was Ivy herself I was fucking. Fuck. I should have taken her while she was here. Shoved her down on her knees and had her suck my cock. She was a Gilligan, and I should hate her. I could have taken that rage out on her pretty little mouth and sent her home to her family ruined, as a message of just what I was capable of when you fucked with the Wynters. But I doubted she was responsible for anything either her father or brothers had done, and the crazy thing was that I didn't want her to think badly of me.

I wanted Ivy Gilligan to like me.

Heat and tension built inside me, my blood rushing through my veins. I could only hear the thud of my pulse and my heavy breaths. My head was filled with an image of Ivy that I'd never seen in real life, of her lying on her back, her hands on those plump tits, her thighs spread for me. Fuck.

I came in a rush of adrenaline, my hips jerking into her dress, spilling myself onto the material. My orgasm slowly faded, and I caught my breath, my heart rate decelerating.

The dress was wet with my cum, and I balled it up in my fist. I should probably toss it back in the bin, but I couldn't bring myself to get rid of it. Instead, I carried it into my room and pushed it between the mattress and the base.

Now I had that out of my system, I took a quick shower and dressed.

I had to take what I'd learned to the other half of our business. I hated sharing things with the Cornells, but it was what my father had wanted, and while he'd had issues with them as well, he'd done what was right for both the family and the business. There was no denying we were stronger together. I believed that was why the Gilligans had been forced to take such extreme steps as setting the bomb.

Taking the elevator down to the private parking garage under the building, I debated on whether I should take my father's black Range Rover or my motorbike. I was doing what I could to ensure people took me seriously, and the car was definitely more grown-up, but the bike got me through the city faster and was a lot more fun.

Fuck it. I was taking the bike.

The roar of the engine turned heads as I left the hotel parking garage, though no one would know my identity due to the helmet jammed down over my skull. I rode skilfully, weaving through traffic, smirking at the irritated glances I received from car drivers who weren't going anywhere.

In less than half an hour, I reached Tam Cornell's Greenwich house—and my sister's place, too, since they were married now—and stopped outside the gate. I leaned in to press the buzzer, fully aware they had cameras and speakers out here. After the attack at the warehouse, none of us were taking any chances.

Whoever was on the other side of the camera clearly knew who I was, as a second later, the electric gates slid open. I got the bike going again, riding more slowly this time to where both Hallie and Tam's four-by-fours were parked outside, sliding the bike neatly between them. I climbed off, dragged the helmet off my head, and hung it on the handlebar. I raked my fingers through my hair, as of yet unused to how short it now was. I missed it being longer, but this was all part of growing up, of having arseholes like Tam taking me seriously.

The front door opened, and my sister appeared in the doorway. She was huge, but I would never say that out loud, at least I wouldn't unless I wanted her to smack me around the back of the head. I might be heading up the Wynter Syndicate now, but she would always be my big sister.

Big sister.

I'd have to remember to avoid calling her that, too.

"This is an unexpected visit," she said, taking a step towards me. "To what do we owe the honour?"

"I need to speak to your husband."

"And me, too, I assume."

Hallie might be massively pregnant, but she still didn't want to be sidelined. I knew she drove Tam crazy wanting to be involved. Our business was dangerous, and Tam's instinct was to protect Hallie and their unborn child, and Hallie raged against it. She'd never wanted to be controlled, despite what our father had been like, or maybe because of it, but I knew she wouldn't put the baby at risk either.

My sister stared at me, her eyes widening. "What did you do to yourself?"

She hadn't seen me since I'd had the style change. "I figured since I'm now the head of the family, I needed to start looking the part."

"I've never seen you in a suit. And what did you do to your hair?"

It still wasn't exactly short, but the jaw-length locks were a thing of the past.

"I cut it, obviously."

Her lips thinned. "You seem older."

"Good."

My youth was one thing that was going to go against me, or perhaps I could make it work for me instead. I didn't like the idea of not having any respect simply because of my age. The prospect pissed me off.

I couldn't help making a comment on her size. "You're...round."

Her hand went to her belly. "Gee, thanks."

"Well, you do have a whole other person in there."

"Not for too much longer, I hope. Only another few weeks to go."

Hallie was a Cornell now, and I hadn't exactly always got along with her husband, Tam. It made me uneasy. My father's decision to join our families hadn't taken into account the possibility of his death. With him gone, the Wynter family was now almost non-existent. Hallie insisted she was still one of us, but how could that be when she was married to a Cornell and was about to birth another one, too, adding to their number?

That was what I needed. A woman to put a baby in her belly. I needed to create a family of my own now. A legacy. I was old enough. I was financially secure. I pictured a faceless woman's belly growing round with my child, and then her birthing it, and, as soon as she was ready, I'd put another baby inside her.

I'd raise sons of my own—many, many sons—and build our empire again. It wouldn't help in the short term, but it would continue our family name.

I knew plenty of women, though most were more like girls and in no way would make good mothers. It was breeding stock

I was looking for and not some simpering teenage girl more focused on makeup and clothes than raising a family.

To my surprise, Ivy Gilligan's face popped into my mind.

No, that was not a good idea at all.

"You'd better come in then," Hallie said.

I loved my sister. Hallie was probably one of the only people left in this world who I had genuine love for. I hadn't been happy for her to marry into the Cornell family, but my father had insisted it was the right thing to do. He'd been the boss then, and both Hallie and I knew better than to question him. Of course, that didn't mean we'd never fought with him—of course we had—but when it came to business, he got the final word.

Now he was gone, and the final word was mine.

His men were my men now. Rumblings among them left me uneasy, but I didn't think any of them would be stupid enough to cross me. They didn't like taking orders from someone so much younger, however. I knew how they'd seen me—the wild, fun-loving one, who never took anything seriously and loved drinking and picking up as many women as possible. Our father had encouraged it, too. I think he'd lived vicariously through me, remembering what it had been like when he was younger and didn't have the responsibilities of the family on his shoulders. I felt bad for Hallie for never getting to experience that. She never would now, and when she became a mother, she'd have even more responsibility. Maybe, when she reached forty, she'd go wild then. I found myself smirking at the idea. Tam Cornell wasn't far off that age now. Would his younger wife leave him behind eventually?

Hallie led me into the house and shut the door behind me. The big gates I'd driven through had also swung shut and automatically locked. Security was important.

"Tam," she called out as we walked through the house. "Jay's here."

Tam Cornell emerged from his office, twin lines between his brows. He was always so serious. It wouldn't do him any harm to smile occasionally.

"I got a name out of one of the Gilligans' men last night," I said. "Does the name Doyle mean anything to you?

His eyebrows furrowed deeper. "Doyle? Is that a first name or surname?"

"I assumed surname. You haven't heard it before?"

"It doesn't ring any bells, but I'll ask around."

"Why would someone we've never heard of order an attack on the warehouse?"

Tam's eyes narrowed slightly. "Does that mean you've changed your mind about the Gilligans being the ones responsible?"

I couldn't help my thoughts going to Ivy. She hadn't exactly stuck up for her family name either.

"No. He could just be someone who works for them."

"To order a hit of that level? I'd expect something like that to come from the top."

"It could be a way of the Gilligans protecting themselves," I suggested. "Adding another layer of defence. They know if we find out for sure that they did this thing, it'll be enough for full-on war."

Tam arched an eyebrow. "I thought that's what you were waging anyway."

The truth was that I wanted to be king here, but Hallie's marriage to Tam complicated things. I didn't want to share my throne, and I hated that, with Tam being the eldest, even in his own family, he ruled the roost. His brother, Leo, seemed content to live the easy life with Kaja and let Tam lead the way, but I wasn't going to sit back and take things so easily.

"I've got a meeting this afternoon with a potential new supplier," I told Tam. "I think we'll be able to undercut what the Gilligans are bringing in substantially, so we can bring some of their business over our way."

"You want to move onto their turf?"

North London had some boroughs with serious money. It would be an area worth having.

"I don't just want to move onto their turf, I want to turn them off it and piss all over it to mark my territory. Since we're in this together now, I assume I have your support."

Tam cocked his head. "Let's see if we can make the deal first."

If the Gilligans left North London, what would happen to Ivy? She'd have to go with them. She'd be too exposed living alone without the protection of her family. Would that mean I'd never see her again? I'd secretly hoped I might bump into her by accident in central London sometime soon.

That wouldn't happen if I drove her family out of the city.

Chapter Six

Ivy

It had just gone eight p.m. as I stood outside the hotel in Shoreditch. Someone tried to get past me, walking at a brisk pace, pulling a wheeled suitcase along behind them. I apologised and darted out of the way. I prayed no one would recognise me and ask me what I was doing here. I was a Gilligan and shouldn't be on this side of the city.

I didn't even know if Jayden would be in. I'd come up with a feeble excuse—wanting my expensive shoes back. He could easily have put them in the post or got a driver to drop them off.

The truth was that I wanted to see him again.

Warning sirens sounded in my head. What good would come of this? Our families were enemies.

Maybe I was thinking about this too deeply? It didn't have to mean anything, did it? I was allowed to just spend time with someone. It wasn't as though I had many friends, and those I did have I suspected only liked me—or pretended to like me—because of who my family was. Growing up in a house full of brothers, I'd struggled to understand how to communicate with girls. The rough and tumble play didn't go down well with the little girls at school. I remembered how they'd cry and run off to tell a teacher, and I'd stand to one side, completely baffled at what I'd done. I'd quickly learned it was better to stand back and keep to myself rather than risking getting in trouble. I was twenty now, but it seemed I'd never quite managed to shake off the habit.

I recognised the same concierge who'd been here in the early hours. The poor man clearly did the night shift. Would he remember me? I thought this might be easier if he did.

With my stomach knotted and my heart all but in my throat, I approached him. He noticed me coming and offered me a polite smile.

"Can I help you?"

"Umm...yes, I hope so. I'm here to see Jayden Wynter."

Any normal person would have his phone number so they could just call him to say they were in the lobby. But I didn't have his number, though I'd gone out during the day and bought a new phone and made sure I cancelled the old one. The pricks who'd attacked me and stolen my bag wouldn't have even been able to get into it—the phone was PIN and fingerprint protected. My mind pulled me unpleasantly towards the memory of what I'd gone through, their hands pawing on me, the way they'd been frighteningly strong, overpowering me. The helplessness had been the worst part, the realisation that my name didn't mean a goddamned thing if the people attacking me didn't know about our family and what they did. Then Jayden had come along, and though, initially, I'd been fearful that he'd be the same, he'd been the opposite. He'd taken care of me, and I'd felt safe with him—something I'd never have predicted.

So now here I was, back again.

Was it because I craved that feeling of being safe? Or was I craving his touch on my skin?

"I'll call up and see if he's free. Can I ask who's calling on him."

"Just say it's Ivy," I said, suddenly self-conscious about using my surname around here.

"Just Ivy?"

"Just Ivy," I confirmed.

He replied with a curt nod and then left me to make the call. I stood, feeling even more awkward than ever. A part of me was tempted to make a run for it, but my feet were rooted to the floor. Though I knew everyone *wasn't* staring at me, I could have sworn I had a flashing neon light announcing that I didn't belong here. Besides, Jayden might not even be in, or worse, he might not be alone. What if he had a woman up there and I was interrupting a date on the pretence of getting my shoes back? I would just about die.

The concierge returned. "He's ready to see you."

"Oh, thank you."

Had I been expecting to be turned away?

I smoothed down my hair and tugged on the hem of my dress. It was baggier than the one I'd left torn in the bin at his place, but it was wraparound, the front plunging nicely, showing off what I considered to be my best assets. Did I want him to notice me? Did I like his attention?

Over my shoulder was a bag containing the clothes I'd borrowed, all clean and folded. I thought returning the clothes wouldn't make me look as shallow as coming all this way just to reclaim my shoes, even if they were worth five hundred quid.

Nerves tumbled in my stomach as I followed the man towards the bank of lifts that Jayden had taken me to during the early hours. The concierge was clearly someone who was trusted, as, once the doors had opened, he used a special key on his belt to send it to the private top floor.

He gave me a final nod and stepped back once more. The door shut, trapping me inside, and it rose up. I sucked in a breath and squeezed my hands into fists at my sides. What would Jayden's reaction be towards me? I hoped he'd be pleased to see me, but he might have decided during the day that he should never have helped a Gilligan.

The lift pinged, and I froze as the door slid open, revealing Jayden Wynter standing on the other side.

His dark hair was damp, as though he'd recently got out of the shower. He was more casually dressed than he'd been the last time, in jeans and a t-shirt that clung to his torso and exposed the tattoos running in sleeves down both arms and across his knuckles. He looked good in a suit, but I liked this more casual dress, too.

I quickly stepped out before the door shut again, trapping me inside. The movement brought me close to Jayden, so there was only a foot between us. I thought he might have stepped back to increase the space, but he didn't even budge. He didn't smile either or seem in any way pleased to see me.

I suddenly regretted my decision to come here. What had I been thinking?

"What's in the bag?" he demanded.

I glanced down at the fabric tote over my shoulder. "Your sister's clothes. They're all clean."

His gaze was fixed on me, his dark brows furrowed. I noticed how his eyes were a curious combination of green and hazel—neither one colour nor the other. He took the bag and tossed it to one side without even checking the contents.

He jerked his chin at me. "Raise your arms."

"I'm sorry?"

"I want to make sure you're not armed."

The thought had never even occurred to me. "Why would I be armed?"

"Your father could be using you."

I blinked. "Using me?"

"To finally put an end to the Wynter family."

My jaw dropped. "You think I might have come here to shoot you?"

"I've given you access to a place no other Gilligan would be allowed. If you'd gone home to your father and brothers and told them what happened last night, they might have decided to use it to their advantage. Now, put your hands up."

He spoke in a tone that wasn't to be disobeyed.

I slowly raised my hands above my head. He stepped in closer, shortening the already small space between us to mere inches. I drew a breath, my skin tingling. The scent of whatever gel he'd used in the shower filled my senses, and I resisted the urge to lean in and press my nose and lips to the side of his neck.

He started under my armpits, felt around my back, then returned to my front and under my breasts, cupping each one as though weighing it. I half expected him to brush my nipples over my dress and I already knew that if he did that, they'd harden for him, the points poking through the material.

"Watch it," I snapped.

The corner of his lips curled in a devilish smile.

He ran his hands lower, over my stomach and hips, around to my bottom. I drew a sharp breath as his hands reached between my legs, his warm palms cupping the skin of my inner thighs. The proximity of his fingers to my pussy was impossible to ignore, and heat gathered low in my belly. I felt myself grow slick. Jesus. Was I this desperate that all it took was for a man's hands to be near my thighs to have me practically stripping off my knickers and throwing them at him?

"I don't have a gun!" I squeaked.

He'd ducked low, so I was looking at the top of his head and his thick, mahogany hair. His face was level with my stomach, and I pictured myself lacing my fingers at the back of his head and pushing him even lower.

"I have to be sure," he said, his fingers still trailing the inside of my thighs.

We both knew perfectly well that if I'd been wearing a leg halter he'd have felt it by now.

I stiffened, my body as taut as an elastic band.

"You could have got your man downstairs to do this," I blurted. "Wouldn't that have been safer? I mean, if I'd really planned to shoot you, I'd have done it already, wouldn't I? The lift door would have opened, and I'd have just shot. I wouldn't give you the time to pat me down."

He grinned up at me, and I smacked his hand away. "Arsehole. You never thought I was going to shoot you."

He straightened "Your family would never ask you to dirty your hands like that."

I pursed my lips. He was right. They wouldn't.

"You've got your sister's clothes back," I said. "If I can get my shoes, I'll be going."

He eyed me curiously. "Is that all you came here for?"

My cheeks heated. "Yes. What else would I be here for?"

He studied my face, and I felt myself shrink. Why had I come here? Because he'd made me feel safe, away from my family for the first time. Because I couldn't breathe around them, and I couldn't breathe around him either, but in a completely different way.

"What if I refuse to give you your shoes?"

"Then I guess you'll just get to keep them."

I spun back to the lift, hoping it would work if I just stepped inside and hit the button. I didn't want to stand there like an idiot, waiting for him to use the special key. But no, surely that would be a safety hazard.

I didn't get the chance to find out. A hand caught my wrist and pulled me back around.

"Relax, Ivy, I'm only messing with you."

"You're not funny."

He cocked his head. "So I've heard." There was a teasing in his tone. "Stay. Have a drink with me."

"Don't you have plans?"

He shrugged. "Nothing that can't wait."

This was what I wanted, wasn't it? Even if I hadn't been able to admit it to myself. Ever since he'd dropped me off at the university campus first thing, I'd wanted to be back in his presence again.

"Okay," I relented.

He nodded and turned, walking deeper into the penthouse. He didn't ask me what I wanted but went to the wine fridge in the kitchen, selected a bottle of champagne, and popped the bottle open.

"Are we celebrating something?" I asked.

"You being here."

The heat in my cheeks grew stronger. "Oh, right."

He poured two glasses and handed one to me. We clinked the glasses together.

"*Do* any of your family know you're here?" he asked.

"God, no. They'd lose their shit."

He chuckled. "Good to know."

Was this like an extra 'fuck you' to my family? He might not even like me, but having me here was worth putting up with my company if it meant pissing off my father and brothers.

I took a sip of the champagne, the bubbles affecting the back of my nose. The liquid was cold and dry, and delicious. I'd have to be careful how much I drank, or I'd lose my inhibitions.

Maybe that was what he wanted.

He gestured for me to sit on his leather sofa.

"Did you manage to get home without anyone asking any questions?"

I nodded. "Yeah, the plan worked. One of the guys at uni was asking some questions, but I managed to brush him off."

"What guy?" His lips thinned, his eyes hardening.

I shook my head. "No one important."

Was that jealousy I saw in his expression? No, he had no reason to be jealous. It wasn't as though there was anything between us. We hadn't so much as kissed.

"I got a new phone," I said, trying to change the subject. "I was able to keep my same number."

"I wouldn't know what that was."

"Oh, right. You never had my number."

He put his hand out for my phone. "Unlock it for me, and I'll put mine in. Then I'll message myself so I have your number."

I'd thought earlier that this would be far easier if we'd exchanged numbers. I pulled my new iPhone from my bag, unlocked it, and handed it to him.

He frowned down at it for a minute, plugging numbers into the phone, and then handed it back to me. "I'm under J."

I smiled. "Thanks." It was better that I didn't have his full name in my phone in case my father decided to check it.

We fell silent for a moment.

"I'm sorry about your dad," I blurted.

It seemed like the right thing to say, and I'd wanted to break the quiet. It hadn't been that long since he'd been killed, and I'd have said the same thing to anyone who'd recently lost someone they loved.

He shook his head and glanced away. "I don't want to talk about that. I especially don't want to talk about it with you."

"Why? Because I'm a Gilligan?" His lack of a response was enough to tell me I was right. "I didn't have anything to do with his death, Jayden. You must know that. I'm not my family, and even if I was, you don't know that they ordered his death."

A muscle in his jaw twitched. "I said I didn't want to talk about it, Ivy."

I needed to respect that, even though I wanted to plead my case. It didn't seem fair that he'd blame me, at least in part, for something that had nothing to do with me.

To hide my awkwardness, I took a couple of swigs of my champagne. The alcohol had started to blur the edges of my mind, and I relaxed into it. I'd rather be slightly tipsy with him than sitting here feeling completely out of place.

Jayden knocked back the rest of his drink and then topped up our glasses. At least he wasn't asking me to leave.

"How's the head?" he asked.

I glanced down and self-consciously raised my fingers to the plaster. "Oh, it's fine. A bit sore but not too bad."

"Can I look?"

"There's not much to see."

He raised his eyebrows, and I knew he wasn't going to take no for an answer. I set down my glass and exhaled a breath.

He edged closer, so the side of his thigh pressed to mine. I was so conscious of his proximity, every nerve ending across my skin seemed to be alight.

"It can't have been easy, going through what you did last night." His fingers were still at my temple, his body impossibly close, his thigh burning against mine. "Plenty of people—women and men—would have lost their shit, but you were brave."

"No, I wasn't."

"Yes, you were, and when I patched you up, you didn't complain. You were such a good girl."

A flush of heat rushed through my body. My breath caught, and my nipples hardened beneath my top.

Jesus, fuck. What the hell was that?

A tingling flared between my thighs.

Hell, no. I was not going to be responding in that way to Jayden Wynter.

But longing filled me. "Say it again."

He glanced down at me. "What?"

My voice was breathy, and I could barely believe I was saying this out loud, but my desire was stronger than my embarrassment. "Tell me I'm a good girl."

His fingers pushed back my hair. "You're such a good girl, Ivy."

His cock was clearly outlined in his jeans. God, he looked big. I wanted to touch him. I wanted to taste him. Was it just because he was out of bounds? Or maybe he wasn't the only one who wanted to give a 'fuck you' to my family. Maybe I was doing the same thing myself?

His fingers trailed from my hair, tracing my jaw, and then running down my throat. I found myself tilting my head to one side, giving him more space. He moved farther downwards, leaving a rash of goosebumps in his wake. I sighed and leaned in closer, wanting more. He obliged, his hand reaching my shoulder and slipping under the strap of my dress. Unlike last night, I wore a bra, but that didn't seem to slow him down at all. He slipped both the straps of my dress and the bra down my shoulder and then lowered his head and placed his lips against the spot where they'd been.

This was crazy. He was a Wynter, and I was a Gilligan, and we were enemies. But right now, I suspected we'd both forgotten which families we belonged to.

His palm brushed my breast, and my nipple tightened. He dropped lower, tugging my dress down, together with my bra, and cupped my tit to raise the nipple to his mouth. He covered me with his lips and tongue, sucking and squeezing, grazing his teeth over the sensitive flesh.

"Oh God."

Arousal coiled tighter in my pussy, and I squeezed my thighs together. I wanted more, hungry for it, but the tiny, sensible part of my brain that still existed blared a warning.

This was Jayden Wynter. He was known to be a complete man-whore. How many women had he taken on this sofa? I was making myself another notch in his bedpost.

He pulled down the other side of my dress, freeing my other breast to the air. He moved to feast on them as though he was starving, and before I realised what was happening, I found him pushing me with his body so I was lying on my back, with him over me. I should tell him to stop, but God, his mouth felt good on me.

"You have such pretty tits, Ivy," he told me between sucks and licks. "Anyone ever tell you that before?"

Breathless, I shook my head. No one had ever told me because I'd never let anyone close enough. Here was me, a twenty-year-old virgin with a total male-slut. Only one of us was going to get hurt here, and it was bound to be me.

He continued to suckle on me. His mouth felt incredible on my nipples—I had no idea they could be so sensitive—and it was as though they had a direct line to my pussy. I definitely got the impression he was a boob man. He jammed his hardness against me, and I ground against it, the sensations it caused leaving me spinning, like I was drunk, though I'd only had a couple of mouthfuls of champagne. I loved the way he spoke to me, though. What was with that? It did strange things to me I'd never experience before.

His hand found its way under my dress, his fingers skimming my G-string. It was sopping wet, and he'd barely touched me.

"So wet for me. Your pussy wants me, Ivy."

"Jayden, wait," I gasped.

He applied pressure to my clit over the top of my underwear, and my hips bucked into his hand.

If I didn't stop this now, I was going to lose my moment. I opened my mouth to speak, but then he was kissing me again, his tongue sliding across mine. I responded, lacing my fingers through his hair. He nibbled on my lower lip, catching it between his teeth, hard enough to hurt but not badly.

I shoved at his shoulders. "No, wait, stop."

He didn't stop, and I was so tempted to let him do whatever he wanted to me. Desire had caught me in its grip, and I so badly wanted to chase my arousal all the way to orgasm.

But if I let this continue, there was no going back.

I twisted my face away, breaking the kiss. "Jay, no. I said stop."

He removed his hand from my pussy. "What's the matter? Aren't you comfortable? We can go to my room."

I shook my head. "I'm sorry, Jay. I should go."

Chapter Seven
Jayden

Fuck.

I sat up, my cock straining against the front of my jeans. "What?"

"I have to go."

"Now?"

Was she joking?

She yanked up the front of her dress, cupping those perfect tits back in her bra, hiding them from my view. It was sacrilege to keep them hidden.

"Yes, I'm sorry. I really should go."

I tried to process what had just happened. "Why? Because we were making out?"

Her cheeks flushed a pretty shade of pink. Her lips were swollen from the kisses and still wet. I wanted nothing more than to cover her with my body and feast on every inch of her skin.

"Why did you come here if this isn't what you wanted?"

She didn't meet my eye. "I came here to give your sister's clothes back and to pick up my shoes."

"I didn't give a fuck about Hallie's clothes, and you could have sent someone round for the shoes or I could have had a courier send them over."

Her tongue flicked across her lower lip. "I didn't want anyone to know I'd been here."

I set my jaw. "Bullshit. Tell me why you really came."

"I-I don't know. I just wanted to see you."

"Because you wanted this." I motioned between us. *Whatever this was.*

Her eyes widened. "No!" But then she glanced away. "Yes...maybe."

How could she deny the chemistry between us? I was as surprised as she was. While I didn't hold her responsible for the wrongs her family had caused me, the last person I'd ever wanted to get involved with was a Gilligan. I should ask her to leave and cut off all ties now, but I couldn't bring myself to do it. I'd got a taste of her and discovered I wanted more.

Maybe it was just because of who she was that left me feeling this way.

Was it because she was the one unattainable person in my life, and that's the reason I wanted her?

Ivy climbed off the sofa. "I still should go. In fact, this"—she waved between us in the same way I'd done moments before—"is even more reason for me to go. It can't happen. It just can't. We're from two opposite sides of the track."

"Hallie and Tam work," I pointed out.

"They made an alliance, you know that." She arched an eyebrow. "Are you going to make a pact with my father?"

I started back at her suggestion. "Fuck, no."

She shrugged and moved even farther away from me. "Well, there you go then."

My cock ached. I wanted her so badly, but at what cost? There was no chance I was going to come to some sort of agreement with a man I believed responsible for murdering my father.

"What about you?" I threw out there. "You could be the one to walk away from your family."

It was a ridiculous suggestion, and I knew it the moment the words came out of my mouth. How could I ask her to do such a thing, and for what? Just so I could get my dick wet? Why the hell would she ever agree?

Ivy clearly thought the same.

"What is it you want from me, Jay? It's just sex, right? You're lonely, and I like how you make me feel. But let's not pretend this is going to lead to anything. We're both young, and if you think I'm going to betray my whole family for a fuck, you're greatly mistaken."

Ouch. I was too proud to admit it to her, but that stung.

"I haven't asked you for anything," I said.

She tilted her head. "Just for me to spread my legs."

"You seemed to be enjoying what I was doing to you. There were no worries about your family name when you were asking me to call you a good girl."

Her cheeks flared red. "Don't you dare try to shame me for it. How many women have you had sex with, huh? I bet you've had a hell of a lot more women than I've had men, so you don't even get to *think* that I'm the easy one."

She had a point. From the age of fifteen, once I'd realised how attractive the combination of my name, money, and looks made me, I hadn't held back. I'd fucked my way through my teenage years, growing irritated with any woman who ever showed any sign of wanting to hang around.

Was I thinking differently of Ivy? Did I want her hanging around?

I mused on the possibility for a moment. She did seem to be occupying a hell of a lot of my headspace at the moment. When I wasn't with her, I was thinking about her. But wasn't that more down to my loneliness than anything else? If my father was still alive, and I wasn't bouncing around in this great big apartment all alone most of the time, would I have even given her a second thought?

I wanted her, though. Fuck. I wanted her. My wrist was aching from the amount of time I'd spent jerking myself off while thinking about her. It was like my whole being was consumed with getting my cock inside her tight little cunt.

Maybe that explained these feelings. It had nothing to do with actually wanting to spend time with her and everything to do with her being a challenge. While there was clearly chemistry between us, she hadn't thrown herself at me, as I was used to women doing. Maybe when I eventually got to fuck her, I'd get all of this out of my system, and I'd finally have space in my head for something that wasn't her.

Something that wasn't her laugh or the scent of her hair or the cute pout she did when she didn't get her own way.

My chest instantly felt hollow at the possibility.

It was just lust, that was all. Something I needed to get out of my system.

But it didn't look as though that was going to happen tonight.

Ivy was back on her feet, gathering up her belongings.

"Don't go," I said. "I want you to stay."

"Why? So you can get in my knickers?"

I put up both hands. "I'm not going to pretend I don't want to, but I also want to just be in your company. I want to get to know you."

She snorted, clearly not believing me.

"Okay," I said, wanting to prove my point, "if you could only eat one kind of food for the rest of your life, what would it be?"

She narrowed her eyes at me and folded her arms over her chest. Attitude exuded from every pore, but she answered.

"Thai. Hot as I can get it."

"Interesting. If you had an evening to yourself, what would you do with it?"

"I'd go to the cinema, on my own, and sit at the back with a tons of snacks, and watch whatever I wanted."

"You like films then?" I checked.

"I like all forms of fiction, whether they're films or books. I prefer them to real life."

Fair enough. There were plenty of times when I wished I could vanish from reality.

She stared at me, a challenge in her eyes. "Anything else?"

"Did your family have anything to do with Harvey Cornell's murder?"

Shit. Where did that come from?

Her lips thinned, and for a moment I didn't think she was going to reply, but then she shook her head.

"Are we just your general get-out cause? Blame everything on the Gilligans so you don't need to worry about either searching farther afield or maybe even closer to home?"

"I guess it's just that if something looks like shit and smells like shit, it's normally shit."

I'd taken things too far.

Ivy turned away from me. "Goodnight, Jayden."

Considering I'd wanted to keep her around, I hadn't done a very good job of it. I considered calling her back again but changed my mind. Ivy might be leaving my penthouse, but she wouldn't be leaving the city anytime soon. I had ways of tracking her down again. It was probably best to do so after she'd calmed down.

She reached the lift and punched the button without facing me. She must have forgotten that her face was reflected in the mirrored walls, however, and I could see how red she was and that her eyes were glassy. She was upset, but whether it was anger or misery, I couldn't quite tell.

The doors slid shut, closing her off from my view.

I sighed and sat back.

What exactly was I planning to achieve by screwing with Ivy Gilligan? Despite what she'd said, it wasn't all about sex, was it?

Could I use her to help me find out who'd ordered the hit on my father? I didn't want her to pity me, but if I could make her feel something for me, then maybe she'd want to help me. A twist of guilt went through me at the thought of using her like that. I had to remind myself that she was a Gilligan. I wanted to destroy her family. She'd been a fool for coming to me in the first place.

But this was a war, and there were always going to be casualties.

Chapter Eight

Ivy

Days passed, and I managed to stay away from Jayden Wynter.

Only physically, though.

In my head, I was living on his sofa, with him between my thighs and his mouth on mine, or his lips trailing down my neck, or covering my nipple. Every time I remembered how he'd called me a good girl and how I'd made him repeat it, a tingling rush of heat flared to life inside me. I'd got a taste and now I wanted more, however much I knew it was a bad idea.

I went to my lectures and tried to focus on what the tutors said. I had my finals this year, and while I was confident I'd pass, I still wanted to do the best I could. My education would be my ticket to a different kind of life. I didn't want to spend my life worrying about who might have killed whom, and what parts of the city I was allowed in, or worry about who I might be seen with.

I wanted to be free from it all.

The secret I carried with me was a weight on my shoulders. I wanted to unburden myself from it, but I still hadn't figured out how to do that without creating another war. But those affected had the right to know, and I'd been testing the waters on that front. I felt sure there was a way for it to happen without any more lives being lost, but that could be a big ask.

As I left my final lecture for the day, I was conscious of someone catching up to me from behind. I glanced over my shoulder to find Kyle almost at my side.

"Hey, Ivy," he said, "are you coming to the pub later?"

I kept walking. "No, I don't think so."

"Why not? The whole gang's going to be there. It'll be fun."

The whole gang? I wasn't sure I was even part of a gang.

But I'd been telling myself for the past couple of days that if I wanted a normal life, I needed to start acting like a normal person. I needed to have regular friends—not people who imported weapons and counterfeit money for a living, or who carried guns, or who lived in the penthouses of multi-million-pound hotels. I didn't want to have to think about who was warring with who, or who might have been responsible for murdering someone else's father.

And I especially didn't want to think about a dark-haired, tattooed man who looked as comfortable in torn jeans and a t-shirt as he did in a suit worth a regular person's mortgage payment.

"What time are you meeting?" I asked.

His eyes brightened. "Eight."

I nodded. "Okay. I might see you later then."

He was like a puppy who'd just been given a treat. "Yeah, great. See you later."

I had absolutely no interest in Kyle, and I hoped I hadn't given him the wrong idea. But it wasn't as though it would just be the two of us—everyone would be there. I hadn't needed to ask which pub to meet at because everyone always met at the Green Lion over the road. It was a typical hangout for students—you could taste the savings in what they served.

He bounded off, and I sighed.

***

I pushed into the busy pub, anxiously glancing around for familiar faces. The odour of stale beer hit me, together with the wall of noise of people talking and laughing. Somewhere in the background music played, but the sound of people was too loud for me to recognise the song. This was a typical student pub—cheap alcohol and zero pretences. The padded, fabric bench seating still had holes from cigarette burns—remnants of the days when people were allowed to smoke inside. I was grateful such a thing was frowned upon now. I didn't want my eyes stinging and my clothes stinking of smoke.

I recognised a couple of faces, but no one I considered myself friends with—or even acquaintances. I managed to make my cheeks tweak in a polite smile, while I fought the urge to run away. Why had I come here again? Oh, yes, to feel normal. Was such a thing even possible?

I was going to need a drink if I was ever going to relax, so I headed straight for the bar. It gave me something to do, too, so I didn't feel so awkward just standing there. I squeezed in between some other people, who were only propping the bar up rather than waiting to be served.

The barman jerked his chin at me, silently asking me what I wanted. I raised my voice to be heard above the din.

"Vodka tonic, please."

"Single? Double?"

"Better make it a double."

I had the feeling I was going to need it. He brought me my drink, and I tapped my card on the handheld machine to pay. Clutching my vodka and tonic, I turned to face the pub again. I took a large gulp of my drink then fished in my bag for my new phone. I was able to automatically update it to have all my contacts and apps, so I didn't miss my old one too much. I hoped those pricks who'd attacked me had never managed to get it unlocked.

I resisted the urge to scroll down to where Jayden had inputted his number under 'J'. I thought I might have heard from him, if only in the form of a text, but it had been radio silence. I probably should have deleted the number to prevent myself from ever drunk dialling him, but I couldn't bring myself to do it.

Why couldn't I? Did I really want to hear from him? Like I'd already told him, nothing could come of this. Maybe I was thinking too deeply into it, but I wasn't someone who just had sex to enjoy it, and then never thought of the other person again. Physical intimacy sparked emotions in me, and I didn't think I could separate the two.

To my relief, Kyle and a few others entered the pub. I straightened and fixed a smile on my face. At least I wouldn't be alone now.

He spotted me, lifting his hand in a half wave, and headed over.

"Hey, you made it," he said.

"Yeah. Decided I could use that drink after all." I raised my glass as though to prove the fact.

"You know Sophie and Dana, don't you?" He introduced the two girls he'd arrived with. Two other guys had spotted us and meandered over, and he introduced them as well. "And Chris and Adam?"

"Of course." I'd been at uni with them all for over two years now. I knew their names and faces, but nothing about who they were as people. I tended to go into class, keep my head down, do my work, and leave again.

Kyle clapped. "Right, let's get some shots in. Get this party started."

I shook my head. "Oh, no. I'm fine. I've got a double in here."

"Another double coming straight up then," he declared.

Everyone cheered, and I didn't want to seem like the loser in the group, so I went with it. Jesus, I was in my twenties now, not a teenager anymore. I should be strong enough to say no to a drink I didn't want. But it was like being caught up in a river, and it was easier to go along with things than fight against the flow, so I found myself with a shot glass in my hand and joining in when everyone clinked theirs together and downed the shot in one.

Aniseed burned my throat and the back of my palate. Sambuca. Yuck. I did my best not to grimace.

Around me, everyone cheered again.

One of the girls looped her arm through mine and started chatting about my outfit and how she loved my bag. I was relieved to be on familiar territory, and the alcohol worked its way through my system, relaxing me. I could do this. I could be a normal student, not someone who had grown up with a family embroiled in crime, and I could enjoy it. How else was I going to learn to be a normal member of society and not some Mafia princess?

We found a table and squashed around it. Kyle had the seat next to me, and it was impossible not to notice how his shoulder, leg, and hip were jammed against mine. Everyone was the same, though; there wasn't much room, so it wasn't as though he was doing it on purpose. I did my best to ignore it and join in on the conversation whenever I found an opening. I hated feeling like I wasn't a part of things, but the only way I was going to fit in was by doing stuff like this.

I drank my vodka and tonic too quickly and stood to get another. The booze had already gone to my head, but I could handle it. I was relieved to be away from the table, if only for a short while, to get some space and not have to feel like I had to talk for a while.

At the bar, I checked my phone. I was relieved to see it was almost half nine. Time had gone quickly, and I thought I'd get away with having one more drink and then heading home.

I bought another double vodka and tonic and carried it back to the table to retake my seat. Kyle offered me a grin and lifted his beer glass to clink it to mine. I tried to absorb myself back into the conversation, but the pub seemed to have grown louder since I'd gone to the bar, and I struggled to pick up on what everyone was saying. I finished my drink too fast again and checked my phone again for a distraction. It was almost ten now. Surely I'd get away with leaving without looking like a party pooper.

Carefully, I got to my feet. Several sets of eyes followed me, including Kyle's.

"You getting another drink?" he asked. "I'll buy you one."

I imagined I had far more money in the bank than he did, though I guessed it was nice of him to offer. "No, I'm fine, thanks. I need to get home now. That sambuca went right to my head." I threw a smile at the others who were also looking my way.

Kyle got to his feet, too. "Stay for one more. It's still early."

"Really, I've had enough."

I'd already taken a couple of steps away from the table, putting some space between myself and the others. But instead of letting me go, Kyle came with me. He positioned himself between me and the door, so the bar was behind me, and he was blocking the way.

"Just one more," he insisted. "You can have a soft drink, if you want."

A spark of anger flared through me. "Oh, can I? That's kind of you to give me permission."

He blinked at my words, surprised that I'd dared speak to him like that. But he had no idea of the background I came from—probably didn't even know that world existed in his simple one of clubbing and Netflix and pulling girls.

"That wasn't—"

Behind Kyle, the pub door opened and shut, and a hush fell over the place as though we were in some kind of Western film and a stranger had just walked in. I glanced over his shoulder and drew a breath. Across the pub, Jayden's eyes locked with mine. He didn't smile.

What was he doing here?

Kyle still had his back to the door and had no idea who had just walked in. "—what I was trying to say," he finished.

A hand clamped on his shoulder, and he jumped, and then spun to discover Jayden directly behind him. Jay had about four inches and probably forty pounds of muscle on Kyle, and that was before Kyle had even noticed the neck and knuckle tattoos.

"You appear to be bothering her," Jayden said, his head angled slightly to the right, his intense eyes glinting.

Kyle gawped. "Who the fuck are you?"

"Wrong answer."

Jayden's grip tightened, and he swung Kyle towards the door. The group of people we'd been sitting with burst into voice, but no one actually got up to intervene.

"Hey!" someone shouted.

"What the fuck?" yelled another.

My face burned. "Jay, stop it!"

He shoved Kyle out of the door and onto the street and then turned back to me and put up both hands. "I'm not doing anything."

All I could feel was everyone looking at us. I grabbed his arm and yanked him around the side of the bar and through the door that led into a small corridor behind. Ahead of us were a handful of doors—two for the men's and women's toilets, and a third I assumed led to a stockroom or cellar.

"What are you doing here, Ivy?" Jayden said.

I threw up both hands. "Having a drink with my friends? What does it look like?"

He arched an eyebrow. "That man was your friend?"

"Yeah. He just got a bit carried away, that was all." I thought of something. "How did you even know I was here?"

This was Gilligan territory. Jayden shouldn't even be in this area, but I didn't think someone like him gave a shit about that.

"I might have installed an app on your phone when you gave it to me to put my phone number into."

My eyes widened. "Seriously? You were tracking me?"

He shrugged like it was no big deal. "I wanted to know where you were."

I fished my phone out of my bag, opened it with my thumb print, and shoved it at him. "Take it off. Now."

"No, and don't try to find it. I've got it hidden behind other apps."

"I just got this phone. I don't need to get another one, and I don't need you knowing where I am at all times. It's creepy as fuck."

"You need protecting. Every time I turn my back, some prick of a bloke is trying to get his hand up your skirt."

I folded my arms. "And you think you're any better."

He lowered his head and growled. "I *know* I'm better."

"Why?"

"Because I'm not in this just for the physical side of things. You're in my fucking head, Ivy. I can't stop thinking about you. That's why I had to come here tonight."

My stomach flipped at his words. He'd been thinking about me. Hadn't I been thinking about him, too?

He moved even closer, boxing me in against the wall with his large frame. "Tell me you haven't been thinking about me."

I couldn't lie, but I couldn't say the words out loud either.

He took that as an affirmation and reached up to brush my cheek with his knuckles. "See," he said softly. "I knew it."

I hitched a breath. Where he'd touched me had lit on fire, and instantly, my body wanted more. He'd barely grazed my face, yet I wanted to strip us both naked and climb him like a tree. He was everything I'd hated about my brothers and father, but here I was, desperate for him.

He moved in even closer and pressed his forehead to mine. "I missed you."

My voice was breathy. "You didn't miss me. You don't even know me."

But I'd missed him, too. So stupid.

"I do know you. I know you like expensive shoes and drink vodka and eat spicy food. I know you like to read and watch films. I know you want to educate yourself because you don't want to carry on living a life where you're going to worry whether or not someone you love is going to come home at night."

Everything he'd said was true.

"And that's why this can't happen," I said. "Don't you think I'll worry every single time you leave the house?"

Why was I even thinking this way? There was no future with Jayden Wynter. It simply couldn't happen. And like I'd said, we barely knew each other.

But I didn't stop him when our lips brushed, and I opened mine wider, my tongue reaching for him. His hands threaded into my hair, raking down, stopping to cup my jaw. I melted into him. God, why did he have such an effect on me? No man had ever possessed me the way he did. I barely knew him, and yet he owned me.

The door opened as someone made their way to the toilets, but Jay didn't so much as flinch. He just carried on kissing me as though we were the only people here. His body pressed hard to mine, his muscles crushing me to the wall behind, and I didn't even care. I wound my arms around his neck, kissing him even deeper.

This was a very public display of affection.

He grabbed one of my thighs, hooking it around his hip, while the other hand found my breast. Desire coiled low and hot in my stomach, and I ground on the erection I found jammed firmly against me. Our breathing grew ragged, and I raked my fingers over his scalp, deliberately digging in my nails.

His hand moved down, pushing beneath the waistband of the very casual sweatpants I'd worn out that night and then into my underwear. His fingers scraped against my mons and then down lower still. I was already wet for him, and he pressed on my clit, sending fireworks through me. I groaned into his mouth.

The position of his body hid what he was doing to me from anyone who was passing, but we were still in public. As far as I was aware, the people I'd been drinking with were still sitting around the table, only on the other side of the door, and there was nothing stopping them catching us. What had they made of Jayden arriving here and throwing Kyle out before dragging me off? They were bound to be talking about it. Would they know who he was? It was unlikely, but he still gave the impression of being someone important. He had that 'don't fuck with me' air. I didn't want any of my friends catching us, though, but I still couldn't bring myself to tell him to stop.

He slid his fingers between my folds and plunged one of his digits deep inside me. I gasped and clung to his shoulders, rocking my hips to meet his movements.

"Your pussy feels so good around my fingers, Ivy," he murmured beside my ear. "You're so hot and wet."

He added a second, stretching me around him.

"Do you like that? Tell me that you like."

"Oh God, yes," I gasped. "I like it."

We were going to get caught, I was sure of it, but for some reason that only added to my excitement. I felt how wet I was as his fingers curled inside me. He caught my hair with his other hand, yanking it hard enough to hurt, pulling my head back like a horse with reins, forcing me to look up at him. I was completely in his grip, willing to do anything he told me in that moment.

I let out a whimper, and my eyes slipped shut, rolling with pleasure. His whole hand owned my pussy, his fingers inside me, the ball of his palm positioned to allow me to grind my clit against it.

The heat of my orgasm built, and I chased my peak, but then he slipped his fingers from me and kissed my mouth.

I wilted in disappointment. "No, don't stop."

He straightened my clothes. "You're coming home with me."

"I can't. I'm supposed to be back soon. I'll be missed from the house."

"Then I'll fuck you in my car and drive you home."

My building orgasm ebbed away, replaced by frustration and irritation. "Such a romantic. You can't drive me home. Someone might see us. You're not even supposed to be in this borough."

I was already concerned about someone reporting our heavy make-out session, but this definitely wasn't the sort of place my family or any of their associates would ever come.

"I don't give a fuck if someone sees us," he growled.

"I do. If my father or brothers found out I was...with you, they'd go nuts."

"So let them."

I shook my head. "You don't understand. You don't have anyone else to answer to."

"Neither do you. You're an adult. You can do whatever you want."

I gave a small laugh. "Says someone who has the point of view of a man."

"What's that supposed to mean?"

I folded my arms across my chest protectively. "Was it the same for Hallie? Were the expectations put on her the same as the ones put on you?" I already knew they weren't. It was well known in our society that, up until recently, Jayden Wynter got to screw around as much as he liked, while his sister was used like a piece of property to secure an alliance between the two families. Maybe things worked out okay for her, but that wasn't the point. "I wish things were different in our world, but they're not. You could count on one hand the number of women running our kinds of businesses, compared to the number of men. If my family found out about us, things would end very badly."

"For whom?" he asked.

"Both of us."

He moved in closer again and lowered his tone. "So how about we just make sure they don't find out."

I shivered at his proximity. "What are you saying? That you want there to be an 'us'? Excuse me for thinking you just want to screw the Gilligans' daughter so you can use it against them."

He grew serious. "Ivy, that's not what I'm thinking, I swear it."

I stared into his eyes, wanting to read the truth. "How can I believe that? It's not like you're known for your good morals."

"You'd just have to try me."

I wanted to scream in frustration. God, he was so tempting. I wanted to know how he looked completely naked. I wanted to taste every inch of his skin and watch his expression as he moved inside me. I was so utterly torn.

It was a risk, and I never took risks.

But for some reason, being near Jayden made me lose my head. All I wanted—no, *needed*—was to feel his hands on me and have his mouth on mine. I wanted him to consume me, to make me forget my name.

One time, I told myself. I could fuck him one time and get this out of my system and never go near him again. No one would have to know. Maybe it would be a mistake giving my virginity to Jayden Wynter, but at least I felt confident that he'd know what to do with it.

I caught him by the front of his shirt, fisting the material and yanking him closer. "Take me out to your car."

He grinned, knowing he'd won, and caught up my hand. He pulled me along behind him, long strides taking us out of the rear exit of the pub and straight through into the small car park at the rear. Jayden's black Range Rover stood out amongst all the battered, boy-racer cars and old Minis.

"A Range Rover," I said. "Original."

What was it about these vehicles that people in our business seemed to love so much?

"I prefer my motorbike, but I didn't think it would be practical."

Oh, so this was his plan all along—to find me and get me into the back of his car?

We were kissing before we even reached the vehicle, our tongues tangling, our hands roaming over each other's bodies. He slammed me against the bonnet and lifted me, so I wrapped my legs around his hips. His hand pushed under my top and roughly shoved my bra up as well, so he could get his hands on my bare breasts. My nipples crinkled and tightened, and he pinched them firmly enough to send heat rocketing down between my thighs. I was still wet and slippery from where he'd been fingering me in the pub. I was ready for him.

But he wasn't going to take me out in the open like this. He set me down for a minute and hit the button on his key fob, opening the Range Rover. Then he reached for the rear door and yanked it open.

"In," he commanded.

He shoved me onto the back seat and took a moment to adjust the front ones forwards to give us as much room as possible. Should I be insulted that he was happy to fuck me in the back seat? Maybe it should feel cheap and nasty, but it didn't. It was raw and urgent and passionate.

I lay on my back, my knees bent, while he positioned himself between my legs. He wrestled off my trainers and then my sweatpants and knickers, leaving me bare to him. My top and bra had already been rucked up, so my tits were exposed.

He stared down at me like he'd never seen a naked woman before. "Fuck. You're so perfect, Ivy."

I'd certainly never thought myself to be anything like perfect, but his words made me feel like I was.

He grabbed my ankles and hooked them over his shoulders and dived down to cover my pussy with his mouth. He kissed my bare folds with hungry nibbles and then latched on to my clit. The effect was instant, my back arching, my hips lifting to meet his tongue. Oh God, had I ever felt something so intense before? I moaned and twisted my head from side to side, my body rolling in time with him. He sucked hard on my clit and then dipped his tongue inside me, licking my inner walls. He pushed my thighs wider, so I was forced to place one foot over the back of the driver's seat.

How was it possible for him to get his tongue so deep? It felt like he was fucking me with it.

I wanted him so badly. I yanked at his shirt, wanting to tear it from his body. I needed to feel his skin against mine.

"Has anyone been here before?" he asked, lifting his face from me to watch my expression as he thrust his fingers back inside me. "Are you a virgin, Ivy?"

I was embarrassed to admit it. I wasn't completely inexperienced—there had been a few boys in my teenage years—but none I'd wanted to go the whole way with. None had ignited this fire inside me, though. I'd never been able to work out what all the fuss was about until now.

"I'm a virgin," I whispered.

"And you're happy for me to fuck you right now, on the back seat?"

I didn't want to wait another single second. "Yes, please. I want it."

"Say that again," he said, with a knowing smile, aware he was echoing my words from the other night.

He continued to finger me, staring into my face. His thumb worked in a circle on my clit, the pressure just right.

"I want it," I repeated. "I want you to fuck me, Jay. I want you to take my virginity, right here on the back seat of your car."

"Good girl."

I groaned with pleasure at his words.

He sat up slightly and tugged at the belt on his jeans. From the line beneath the denim, it was clear he wanted me, too. He flipped open the buckle and then worked the button and zipper of his jeans so he could pull them down his narrow hips.

He wasn't wearing any underwear, and his dick sprang out to meet me, as though grateful to finally be free.

I couldn't take my eyes off him.

His cock was perfect. Big, but not scarily so, and the perfect girth. It curved upwards slightly, towards his navel, and the head was smooth and a shade darker. I wanted to study him, to commit every inch of him to memory.

Because this would be a one-time thing, wouldn't it? I couldn't allow it to become anything more. Just the possibility was too dangerous to entertain.

I reached for him, wanting to touch him. He didn't stop me, and I wrapped my fingers around him, giving him a tentative squeeze. Jay sucked in a breath.

"I didn't hurt you?" I checked.

He shook his head. "No, never."

I pumped his cock, feeling the silky soft, hot skin beneath my fingers. God, he was so big and hard. Could I really get him inside me? I knew I was sure as hell going to try.

"Ah, fuck, Ivy." His eyes slipped shut. "You're killing me here. I want to be inside you."

"I want that, too."

He removed himself from my grip and sat back on his heels. He delved into his jeans and took a condom from his back pocket and rolled it down his cock. I watched, fascinated, as he touched himself. God, he was gorgeous. I hated that something as shallow as looks could have me so fascinated. But it wasn't just that, was it? It was who he was and the way he commanded a room. He had the sort of confidence that stopped people in their tracks.

He covered my body with his and touched his nose to mine. "You sure you're ready?"

"Absolutely."

Reaching between us, he took hold of his erection at the base and positioned himself at my entrance. He teased me with the head, rubbing it up and down my slit, and then nudging inside me by just a few millimetres.

"Ah, Jay, that feels good."

He pushed inside me, using one arm to keep himself hovering above me, and then releasing himself with his other hand and grabbing my hip. He slid in an inch or so, slipping through my wet heat. I gasped, shocked at how my pussy stretched for him.

"Fuck, you're so wet," he told me.

He withdrew slightly, and I clung to him, worried he'd somehow changed his mind, but then he thrust back in, his cock even deeper now. He clutched the inside of my thigh, opening my legs even more for him. I glanced down, wanting to see him entering my body. Pink, wet, stretched flesh. God, that was so hot. It was like we were one person, joined together.

He moved even deeper, and a stab of pain hit me. I sucked air over my teeth and winced.

"It's okay. I'm in now," he assured me. "The pain will fade."

He held still inside me, giving my body time to adjust. His lips found mine again, and he kissed me, deep and passionately, and my inner muscles tightened around his cock. Experimentally, I arched my hips, feeling every inch of him. He groaned against my mouth, and then his lips left mine, and he ducked to one of my breasts, sucking and licking and biting my nipple.

"Aah, fuck," I groaned, and his hips moved, pumping into me.

It felt incredible, and liquid heat pooled in my pussy. I rolled my hips to meet his, any pain I'd felt melting away. He grabbed my thigh, holding me in place as he pounded into me.

I panted for breath, my whole body shaking under his. He thumbed my clit, keeping up the fast circles while he thrust hard and fast. I wanted to touch him, but I had to brace my hand against the door to prevent the top of my head being smacked against it.

My whole body tensed. He drove into me, slamming into me hard, my pussy clenching around his cock. I climbed the crest of my orgasm with him. I'd lost all rational thought, the only focus of my mind and body to reach my peak.

Then I did, and I cried out, my body bucking beneath him. I jammed my hand against the door and stars exploded behind my eyelids. He hit me deep and held there, shuddering above and around and inside me.

"Fuck, Ivy. Holy fuck."

We fell together, both breathing hard. My skin was damp with perspiration. He reached between us and disposed of the condom. Then bent his head and licked and sucked at my nipples again.

"Did I tell you that you have the most perfect tits?"

I giggled. "I really don't."

"If you think that, then you're fucking blind."

I closed my eyes, and he laughed, and his mouth was on mine again, kissing me as though he couldn't get enough.

One time, I promised myself.

I already knew I wasn't going to keep that promise.

Chapter Nine
Jayden

I was obsessed.

I literally couldn't get enough of Ivy Gilligan. When I wasn't with her, I thought about her constantly, and when I was with her, I ached, knowing she would have to leave again.

Days turned to weeks, and we took every opportunity we could to sneak around. It was impossible for me to see her at her house—she lived with people who worked for her father—so she came to me at the hotel. The men who worked for me knew to keep their mouths shut, but I still did my best to ensure none of them found out about Ivy's almost constant presence in my bed.

The only one who knew exactly who Ivy was and how often she was with me was the hotel concierge, Fredrick Gadd, but I slipped him some extra money and made sure he understood how important it was for him not to mention her to anyone.

I worried more for Ivy than I did myself, but that didn't stop me keeping things quiet from my family—and from the Cornells as well. There was nothing they could say or do that would make me stop seeing her, but I didn't want the hassle. There was also the possibility they would threaten to tell Ivy's family about us, and I didn't want to take that risk either. Ivy confirmed for me that her father and brothers were not always good people—something that wasn't surprising, considering the business they were in. I didn't want either of us to deal with the repercussions.

I'd given Ivy a key she could use in the hotel that allowed the lift to go all the way up to the penthouse. My family would think I had lost my mind if they knew I had given a Gilligan the key to my home, but they didn't know Ivy. Over the past few weeks, I'd discovered she was the person I trusted most in my life—not including my sister. Ivy was sweet and honest and wore her heart on her sleeve. She was funny and kind, and I literally trusted her with my life. Though she had a key, she didn't use it without running it by me first. She'd never wanted to arrive here, only to discover I wasn't alone, and I wouldn't want her putting herself in any dangerous situations. But it was handy for the times she needed to come over instead of going home, where her family would keep track of her, and I wasn't in.

The lift door slid open, and she stepped out, her blonde curls damp with rain, her laptop bag slung over her shoulder. Though the first night we'd met properly, she'd been in heels and a tiny dress, I'd discovered she was far more comfortable in a pair of Nikes, sweatpants or jeans, and a tight-fitting crop top–that seemed to be her outfit of choice. It looked good on her, showing off her curves and tiny waist.

She smiled that smile I'd come to adore.

"Hey, baby," I greeted her.

I caught her around the waist and pulled her in against me and kissed her mouth.

"Hey, yourself," she said, kissing me back.

It wasn't just the sex I loved—though I did love it—it was the time we spent doing normal things. We sat for hours on the sofa together, watching the films she loved and sharing snacks. We cooked together, ordering in those meal company options where they sent all the ingredients and instructions, so we didn't need to be worried about someone spotting us in a supermarket. We took long baths, with her between my legs, the back of her head resting on my chest; I loved that position. The water made her breasts weightless, so they bobbed on the surface. I couldn't keep my hands off her, using any excuse to soap her down, when in fact, all I wanted was to touch her tits as much as possible. My erection always gave me away, however, and more often than not we ended up fucking, with her on all fours, and the bathwater slopping over the sides.

Neither of us cared. Nothing else mattered when we were together.

The only topic we tried to avoid was anything about our futures. How could we discuss such a thing when it was practically impossible for us to have one? I had my business to run, and she didn't want her family to know about us.

We had no future.

I'd told myself this would burn itself out, but instead the opposite had happened. The more time I spent with her, the more time I *wanted* to spend with her. Any moment of the day where I wasn't in her company felt like a waste, and I was bad-tempered—even more than usual—and frustrated. I thought people would start to notice, but it turned out I'd been this way since my father had died, so no one said anything.

"What have you been up to today?" she asked, "or don't I want to know?"

I had to admit that the fire in my belly for conquering the city had been somewhat put out since she'd come into my life. All my energy was going on her now. But even so, I still wouldn't tell her about any of the business deals I'd put together recently. It wasn't that I didn't trust her—I did—but I wouldn't ever put her in a position that would make things difficult for her at home. I did feel guilty that one of our deals was around encroaching on Gilligan territory, but it was just business, and I hoped she'd understand that.

"I bought you a present."

Her eyes lit up, and I experienced another twinge of guilt that I hadn't bought her jewellery or another pair of the expensive shoes she liked. This was going to be so much more fun, though.

"Close your eyes."

Ivy did as instructed, closing her eyes and putting out both hands. I stared at her. She looked so sweet and innocent, but that was going to change.

I placed a shoe-box-sized parcel into her hands. "Open it."

She glanced down at the present, clearly surprised at the size, too. But she smiled and tore off the paper.

Her lips created an 'O' of surprise as she stared down at my gift.

"You bought me a dildo?"

"It's a lifelike replica of my cock."

She burst out laughing. "You had a dildo made of your own cock and gave it to me as a present?"

"I want you to experience what it's like to be penetrated by two dicks at once, but I couldn't stand the thought of another man's dick being inside you, so I had a second one made of my own."

She arched an eyebrow. "You couldn't just buy me a regular vibrator?"

"It would make me too jealous. It might have been made based on someone else's cock. I don't want you getting pleasure from anyone but me."

She wiggled her fingers. "What about if I pleasure myself?"

"Only if I'm with you," I growled. "And only when I say so, or I'll be jealous of your hands."

"You're crazy."

But she took the dildo out of the box and stroked its length. Blood rushed to my very real dick. While I'd cut off the cock of another man if she touched it, I liked to watch that.

"You ever used any toys, Ivy?" I asked her.

She shrugged. "Not really. I won a small vibrator in a raffle once, but I felt a bit silly using it."

It was my turn to chuckle. "What kind of raffle offers up a vibrator as a prize?"

"You don't want to know."

She continued to stroke the dildo, running her hand up the length, her thumb swiping the head, and drawing her fingers back down to the base just like she would on me.

I'd ordered some lube with it, and it dropped out of the package. I picked it up and showed her the bottle.

"I want to fuck you in the arse while this is in your pussy."

Her eyes widened. "So I'd have two cocks inside me? I'm not sure there's room."

"There will be. I'll take it slow. I want to see you stretched around both me and the dildo. I want to feel how full you are."

"Have you ever done that with another man?" she asked. "Not so much the sleeping together part, but the sharing a girl part? Is that how you know what it feels like?"

I shook my head. "No, Ivy. I don't share."

"Good, because I would have been jealous of any girl you'd done that with."

"Jealous? I didn't think you were the jealous type."

"I'm jealous of every girl you've ever slept with," she admitted. "I wish I was the only one."

"They were nothing. Just dreams to me. They didn't really happen. Not like with you."

She smiled at me again.

I leaned in and kissed her. "Now get your clothes off so I can see how this looks."

She put the dildo down and caught the hem of my t-shirt, dragging it up and over my head. I rid her of her clothes, too, stripping her naked with a surety that came from all the time we'd spent together lately.

When we were both naked, I jerked my chin at the sofa. "Over there."

She lay back on the sofa and spread her thighs. I cleaned the dildo and then opened the tube of lube and applied a good amount to the head and set it aside for a moment. I needed to make sure she was ready first.

"Touch those pretty tits for me, baby. Play with yourself. Make your nipples nice and hard."

She did as I'd asked, cupping her breasts in her palms, pulling and tweaking the nipples with her fingers. Fuck, that was hot.

"That's right," I praised her. "You're doing such a good job. I wish there was milk coming out of these nipples. I'd suck you dry."

I pushed her thighs even farther apart, opening her up so I could stare right into her perfect, pink pussy. I pushed my middle finger inside her, just up to the first knuckle, and held it there, feeling her inner walls trying to clamp around me. She was so hot and wet, I wanted to force my whole fist inside her, but for the moment, I was enjoying watching her squirm.

"Oh God, Jay. Fuck." She arched her hips again, trying to sink down deeper onto my finger.

"Be a good girl, Ivy," I told her. "Hold still."

She stopped squirming but was breathing hard, her lips parted. She stared at me, desperate but almost fearful of this power I held over her.

"Do you like my finger in your tight little cunt?"

"Yes, oh, yes. Give me more, please."

I planned to give her a lot more.

"How about this?"

I sank to the second knuckle and crooked my finger inwards in a come-hither movement. I studied her face for her reaction. My cock strained hard, wanting attention. Her breathing grew ragged, and she arched her hips. I slid my finger back out of her and lifted it to my face. I inhaled the sweet musky scent of her and then put the finger in my mouth and sucked off her arousal.

"Better than champagne," I told her.

I picked up the dildo and rubbed at her pussy with the head. She was always so wet and ready for me, and she probably didn't need the lube, but it never did any harm.

I pushed the toy inside her, and she whimpered.

"How does it feel?"

"Different. Not bad, though." She gasped again. "Actually good."

I slid it deeper, watching her pussy open up to it and pleasure roll across her features. Her lips parted, and her eyes slipped shut, and she twisted her head to the side. I ducked down and kissed her flat stomach, then trailed a line with my tongue down, over her navel, across her mound, to her clit.

"Good girl, Ivy." I hummed against the sensitive nub. "You're taking it so well."

"Oh, Jay," she moaned.

God, she was so slick between her thighs. I covered her clit with my mouth and sucked on it, hard enough to hurt. Her hips bucked, and she let out a squeal.

I licked and sucked while I edged the dildo deeper still. The sounds of her wet cunt and the lube squelched in my ears. I withdrew and thrust back in. Her hips lifted to meet my hand. I moved the dildo faster and faster, fucking her hard with it, while keeping up my attention on her clit. Her thighs and stomach muscles tensed. I massaged one of her breasts with my other hand, playing with her nipple.

But just before I thought she was about to come, I took the toy from her pussy.

"Jay, no. Don't stop."

I held up the lube. "I want to take your arse, Ivy. I want to see you stretched around my dick."

She paled slightly. "Will it hurt?"

"Not if you do what I say."

I pulled her up and flipped her over so she was on her knees. I wanted her riding the dildo while I took her arse.

I planted a kiss to her damp shoulder. "I want to come inside you, baby. Is that okay? I want to feel you around me and I want to watch my cum drip from your hole."

"I wouldn't have to worry about getting pregnant," she said. It wasn't a question.

"No, though if I put a baby in your belly, it would make me the happiest man alive."

She twisted to stare at me over her shoulder. "You can't be serious?"

"Why wouldn't I be serious?"

"I-I don't know," she stammered. "Because we don't have that kind of a future."

"If you got pregnant, we'd have to consider one."

She turned back around, breaking our eye contact. "Stop teasing me, Jay. Fuck me."

She didn't need to ask twice. With my hand on her back, I pushed her to all fours.

"God, you look so sexy in this position." Her arse and the folds of her pussy beneath, both swollen and wet and ready for the taking. "I could fuck you all day every day and never get enough."

I parted her cheeks with my palms and dropped down to tongue her tight little hole.

Ivy jerked away from me. "God, Jay, no. You can't do that."

She seemed horrified, and I took some amused pleasure from it.

"Can't do what? Lick your arsehole?"

"No!"

"I'll do more than just lick it, baby. I'll take all of it."

"I-I don't know if I'm ready for that."

"Don't worry, I'll get you ready."

She relaxed a fraction, and I rimmed her hole and then pushed my tongue inside. She bucked and squealed, but I held her down. I loved every inch of her. When she started to relax again, her breathing growing faster and shallower, I switched out my tongue for a finger. I inserted the tip and she let out that sexy little whimper again.

"I want to stretch your arsehole wide, Ivy. Don't worry, we're going to use plenty of lube. You trust me, don't you, baby? You know I'd never do anything that would hurt you, unless there was pleasure involved, too."

"I trust you."

"Good girl."

I clicked open the top of the lube and applied a good amount to my fingers and her hole. I didn't want to hurt her. I slid my finger back inside, deeper this time, and fingered her a few more times, loosening her up, and then I added a second.

"Fuck, Jay, that burns."

"Breathe. It'll pass."

When I sensed her relaxing again, I slipped my fingers from her and positioned myself behind her.

I nudged my cock against her hole. "Keep breathing, baby. Try not to tense."

I tried again, but once more, she tensed.

"Play with your clit," I told her.

She reached between her legs, doing as she was told, and my cock got even harder. I loved how she always wanted to please me, at least when we were in bed. Outside of the bedroom, she'd happily tell me to go fuck myself if I was in the wrong, and I loved that about her, too.

I gave her a moment then nudged my hips forward. Her arsehole opened around me and swallowed the head of my cock. Fuck, she was tight.

"Your arsehole looks so pretty stretched around my cock," I praised her, knowing how much she liked it. "You're taking me so well."

I went slowly, edging inch after inch, until the whole of my dick was surrounded by her. It took every inch of my strength not to grab both her hips in my hands and pound her hard until I came, but I knew I had to make this good for her if I ever wanted a repeat performance, and fuck, did I want a repeat performance.

When I felt her adjust to me, I started to move, just with small nudges of my hips.

She was ready to take more.

"Are you ready for your pussy to be filled as well?"

She nodded, her breath coming in tiny snatches of air.

Holding my cock deep in her arse, I pulled her back up so she was on her knees again and positioned the dildo I'd had made at her pussy. She was sopping wet, and we'd used plenty of lube, so it pushed inside her easily.

"Oh fuck," she panted. "Oh shit, Jay."

I could feel the movement of the dildo inside her, pressing up against my dick, just a layer of skin and flesh and muscle between us.

I held her tight, her back to my chest. I kissed the sensitive point between her shoulder and neck and licked her sweat. "How does it feel?"

"Like I might lose my mind. I'm so full."

I held the dildo inside her and drew my cock out of her arsehole a few inches, then I plunged back in. Her tits bounced beautifully. God, that was an incredible sight.

I got into a rhythm, fucking her from behind while her pussy pulsed around the toy. Her head fell back onto my shoulder, giving me an even better view of her perfect breasts. I covered one of them with my hand, my forearm crushing the other. I held her so tight, burying my face in her neck, losing myself in her.

There was no way I'd be able to last much longer. The sexy little cries she was making were enough to tip me over the edge. I slammed into her, harder and harder, and then she cried out, shattering beneath me.

A rush of heat and pleasure tightened my balls, and I emptied myself into her, pumping stream after stream of cum. My head spun as the final pulses of pleasure left my body, and I slumped over her back. I was growing soft inside her, but I didn't want to move.

Eventually, I slipped the toy from her body, and we both fell into a heap together. I pushed the dampened strands of her blonde hair from her face. She seemed dazed.

"I meant what I said about wanting that future with you. I think I'm falling in love with you, Ivy."

She twisted her face into my chest, burying herself from me. "No, don't say that."

"Why not?"

I caught her chin, lifting her face again, making her look at me.

"Because we can never make this work, and you know it."

"We can run away. I'll leave my side of the business to Tam."

"What about Hallie? She's going to have her baby any day now. Don't you want to be around to see it?"

My heart contracted at the thought of leaving my sister. Would she ever forgive me?

"Once your family has come around to the idea of us, we can visit."

She blinked back tears. "You don't understand, Jay. They'll never come round. You're a Wynter, and I'm a Gilligan. They'll see it as the worst possible betrayal."

I didn't want to make her cry.

"Hey, I'm not going to force you into doing anything you don't want, okay? We'll figure this out. I'm not sure how, but we will."

I pulled her into my arms and kissed her again. Though it hadn't escaped my notice that when I'd told her I thought I was falling in love with her, she hadn't said the words back.

Chapter Ten
Ivy

I pushed open my front door and stepped into the hallway, tossing my keys on the side. It was late. Mara would have gone to bed already, and I hoped none of my father's men were around. I didn't want to talk to anyone. All I wanted was to relive the sex I was having with Jayden over and over in my head. I'd never experienced anything like it before. The way he touched me and the things he said to me drove me crazy. I basked in his adoration.

He'd said he was falling in love with me, and I hadn't said it back. I hadn't been able to bring myself to. I worried about what admitting such a thing would instigate. And Jesus, he'd even talked about babies. I'd never for one minute thought Jayden Wynter would be the sort of man who'd want to settle down, yet here he was, imagining a future that was impossible for us. Was that why he was talking about it—because he knew it would never happen? Perhaps it was a safe fantasy.

Something was strange—something off and different about the house. There was a weird atmosphere.

I paused. Was someone else here? The place was in darkness. Was it Mara?

I didn't like to walk around armed as I knew my brothers often did, but that didn't mean I didn't know how to fire a gun. There was one attached underneath the top shelf of the hall unit in case of emergencies. I almost wished I'd thought to take it with me the night I was attacked, but you couldn't normally get away with carrying a loaded gun into a nightclub in London—not that it didn't happen, of course.

Before I could give it any more consideration, a light came on farther into the house, and I froze.

"Ivy?"

Confusion rushed through me. That was my father's voice.

"Dad?"

I followed the light into the dining room. To my surprise, it wasn't only my father in there, sitting around the dining room table, but both of my brothers, too. My dad, Greyson Gilligan, was at the head of the table. To his right was my eldest brother, Bruno, and across from Bruno sat Aiden. They all looked deeply serious.

"What are you all doing here?" I asked. "Why are you sitting around in the dark? Did you not want someone to know you were here?"

Who was the someone? Was it me? Why would they not want me to know they were here?

My stomach knotted. This was bad. I could tell.

"Sit down, Ivy," my father said.

I looked at all their faces, trying to read what this was about, but couldn't.

I slid into one of my chairs and placed both hands on the table, as though trying to show them I had nothing to hide.

"Tell me what you're here for. You're frightening me."

My father's lips thinned. "Someone saw you coming out of the Wynter hotel last night."

My stomach lurched. My first instinct was to deny it. "I don't think so."

The lines between his eyebrows deepened. "You're saying they were mistaken?"

"They must have been. Who said they saw me?"

What were any of my father's people doing over in Wynter territory? I guessed they could ask the same of me, but I had a reason for it. The only reasons I could think of were that they were spying on me, or they meant Jayden harm.

He didn't answer my question. "Where were you last night then, Ivy? Where have you been tonight?"

"At the library, studying," I lied.

"It's almost one in the morning."

"The library stays open late, and then I went to get drinks with friends. I'm twenty years old. I can do what I like. I don't need to report myself to you."

He scowled. "Yes, you do, especially when my money is funding your education."

Anger rose inside me. "Then I won't take your money. I'll get a job and a student loan like everyone else."

He gestured around him. "And what about this house? Who do you think paid for that?"

I tightened my hands into fists. "It's in my name. Legally, I own it. And had I known that accepting it would mean you'd get to keep tabs on everything I did, I'd have thought twice."

He linked his fingers together on the tabletop. "Where were you last night, Ivy?" he repeated, clearly not taking my first answer.

"At the library," I insisted.

"And if I check that with the university, they'll be able to confirm it? They'll supply me with CCTV footage of you entering and leaving the building?"

Iced water plunged through my veins. That was never going to happen because I'd never been there. Other than those couple of hours a few weeks ago, I hadn't been anywhere near the library. All my time had been spent with Jayden.

I did my best not to let my emotions show and shrugged. "Do what you like."

I wished I'd chosen a spot that was harder to trace, but this was London—filled with CCTV cameras—and my father had men secreted in every pocket of North London. If he wanted to get his hands on information, he would.

What was I going to do? I'd have to stop seeing Jay—it was my only option. But the thought tore me in two. I didn't want to stop seeing him. I wondered what he would say if I told him that my family suspected us. He would probably say that they'd just have to deal with it then, but he didn't know my family, not like I did. My father expected that the people under him lived by his rules, and there was no way he'd have a daughter fraternising with the enemy.

I sighed as though I was bored by this whole conversation. "Is there anything else you want to interrogate me about 'cause I'm actually really fucking tired from studying all the time. It is my final year, in case you've forgotten."

The men exchanged glances. I sat with my hands in fists, my breath held.

My father jerked his head. "Fine, go to bed. But make sure you are where you say you are from now on."

"I always am," I snapped but got to my feet, relieved to make my escape. "You can see yourselves out."

I turned and stalked out of the room, close to tears and my heart hammering. I hurried up the stairs and slammed into my room, feeling like I was a teenager again. I sat on the end of my bed and waited to hear them leave. It wasn't until I was finally alone again that I allowed myself to breathe.

Fuck, fuck, fuck. I put my head in my hands. What was I going to do? I had no choice, did I? I was going to have to let Jay go.

Without even bothering to undress, I climbed under the covers. Tears slid down my cheeks and dampened the pillow beneath my head. I didn't think I'd ever get to sleep, and I'd just lie there, steeped in misery until the sun rose, but finally, oblivion claimed me.

***

It took me a moment upon waking to remember what had happened.

I couldn't see Jay again.

My soul felt heavy, as though it weighed on my limbs, making it too difficult to get out of bed.

Beside my bed, my phone buzzed. I picked it up, already knowing it would be him.

All I can think about is how you taste. I need to see you.

I stared at the message, desperately wanting to reply. But how could I? If I told him that my family were onto us, and that someone had seen me, he'd just say 'fuck them'. He wouldn't let my family tell us what to do. It was different for him.

I wished I could figure out a way to make myself not care, but I was fearful of what they'd do if it was confirmed I'd been seeing Jayden Wynter.

My phone buzzed again. *I miss your skin against my lips.*

Fuck.

Goosebumps crept up over my neck. I ached for him. I wanted nothing more than to go to him.

My first lecture was at nine, but I already knew I wasn't going to make it. I wasn't going to make it to any of my other lectures today either. In fact, I doubted I'd even get out of bed, unless it was to use the bathroom.

A tear trickled down my cheek, and I swiped it away. My fingers itched to reply or call him, but I couldn't. No good would come of it.

God, I missed him already.

I lay in bed, lost in thought, just letting the minutes tick by.

A knock came at my door, and it opened a crack. The housekeeper stuck her head in.

"Are you unwell, Ivy?" Mara asked. "You've overslept for class."

It was easier to say I was sick than tell the truth.

"I think I've picked up a bug from somewhere."

She frowned and entered the room fully. I twisted my face into the pillow so she didn't notice me crying.

"Don't come too close," I mumbled into the material. "It might be catching, and I don't want to get you ill, too."

I sensed her pause halfway across the room.

"Okay," she said hesitantly. "Can I get you anything? Some paracetamol or something to eat?"

I shook my head. "I just need some more sleep."

"I'll leave you in peace then."

She probably thought I was hungover, though it wasn't normally in my nature to drink too much and stay out late. I *had* been staying out late recently, though. I hoped she hadn't been the one to tip off my father.

My mind was a whirlpool of worries, new ones darting like lightning strikes across it each time they formed. What if my father managed to get hold of my phone records? I had Jayden under 'J', but it wouldn't take much for him to figure it out. Would he be able to see the messages we'd sent back and forth? Would he be able to read them? What about all the calls and how long they'd been? I'd never be able to explain that away. At least I no longer had any tracking apps on my phone—I'd made Jay take off the one he'd installed—though the men in my life preferred it if I did.

The sensible thing would be to delete all the messages, and his number from my phone, and not see him again, but I couldn't bring myself to do it.

God, why was this so hard?

A couple of hours passed, and Jay's messages went from sexy to worried to angry.

Where are you?

Why aren't you replying?

Fucking answer me, Ivy.

In the end, I turned off the phone.

***

A couple of days later, I managed to find the energy to go back into university. I didn't want to talk to anyone, and, even though I'd been sleeping every hour possible, I was still utterly exhausted.

My heart was broken, and more than anything, I wanted Jay to come and put it back together again.

I'd completely lost my appetite, but I needed caffeine more than ever to function. I stopped at one of the high street coffee shops and bought a large latte with a double espresso shot to take away.

As I left the shop, a body blocked my way, and my heart caught. It was his familiar shape, the dark hair and tattoos, his fierce eyes.

Jayden.

He was furious.

"What the fuck is going on, Ivy? Are you ghosting me?"

I couldn't look at him. "I'm sorry. I didn't have any choice."

"There's always a choice."

I shook my head. "Someone saw me outside your hotel the other night. They reported it back to my father."

He dragged his hand through his hair. "Fuck. What did you say?"

"I denied it was me."

"And he believed you?"

"He didn't have any photos or videos, thank God, but yes, I think he believed me. If he hadn't, he would have checked up on where I said I'd been and would quickly have discovered I'd been lying, and that never happened."

"We'll have to be more careful."

I raised both eyebrows. "No, we won't, because this can't happen anymore."

He looked crushed. "You don't want to see me?"

"I mean, I do, but we can't. If my father finds out for sure, he'll kill you."

Jay squared his shoulders. "Let him try."

I sighed. "I knew you'd do this. That's exactly why I didn't message you back."

"Do what?"

"Do the whole macho, bravado bullshit." I glanced from side to side. "Seriously, Jay. I don't even want for us to be seen together here. My father has eyes everywhere. You need to go."

I was still paranoid about who might see us together. No one was around right now, but all it would take was one person. The wrong person. Just one confirmation of a sighting of us together would be enough to prove to my family that they'd been right. I doubted this time they'd forget to take a photo either.

"Fuck that. I want you, Ivy. Screw what your family think. I thought you felt the same way about me. We're meant to be together."

Tears formed in my eyes. "You'll find someone else."

"I don't want anyone else. Is that what you want? Some other man? 'Cause I'll tell you this right now, I'll fucking kill any other man who puts a finger on you. You're mine."

"Jay...stop."

"No. I won't. I'll never stop. I'm not going to allow your family to take you from me. I want you more than I care about your family's opinions."

My heart ached. "If it was just opinions I was worried about, we wouldn't be having this conversation. You're not that naïve, Jay. You know what world we live in."

"Then I'll talk to them, man to man."

He still wasn't getting it.

"They won't just talk," I said. "Someone will get hurt."

He lifted his chin. "It won't be me."

"I'm sorry, but I can't do this, Jay. It was fun while it lasted."

My words seemed to make him even angrier. "Fun? Is that all it was to you? Don't bullshit me, Ivy. I know we were more than that—we *are* more than that. You're important to me. Don't try to act like this meant nothing."

Of course it didn't. Us being together had meant everything to me, but I was frightened about what lay ahead.

"I'm going to be late," I said.

I tried to step past him, but he caught me by the arm and yanked me back again.

"Don't do this, Ivy. Don't leave me. I don't want to go back to a life without you."

I found myself pressed to his chest, the coffee I'd just bought dangerously squashed between us. My forearms pressed against his pectoral muscles as though I was trying to create a barrier between us. Being so physically close to him wavered my resolve. I burned for him. Did he understand this weakness? Was that why he'd come here instead of just trying to call or message me again?

Jay softened his tone. "We'll just be more careful, baby. We can do that. We don't have to stay in the city. We can go anywhere we want."

"I have lectures. I can't go anywhere I want. This is my final year, and I don't want to fuck it up."

"You can go places at the weekends, can't you?"

I wanted it so badly, to be able to carry on seeing him. My entire being yearned for a way to make this work, but my head screamed at me to stop. This was a big mistake. I couldn't make it work. It was impossible. Even if we managed to pull off the whole 'only seeing each other at the weekends' plan, how long could we make that last? At some point, we'd either get caught, or we'd have to break it off, or we'd have to come into the open about our relationship and deal with the fallout, whatever that may be. But still, the siren of finding a way to carry on seeing him sang to me.

"What if they follow me? They're bound to get suspicious if I suddenly start going away every weekend."

He stared at me, and I thought he was trying to come up with an excuse about why I'd be away all the time—a training course somewhere, perhaps, or a part-time job—but then he frowned and shook his head.

"Fuck it, that's not going to work."

Even though he was mimicking what I'd been thinking, that didn't stop my stomach dropping. So, this was it then? We really were going to have to part ways.

But Jayden continued, "Weekends aren't enough for me anyway. I want you all the time, Ivy. Every day. I can't just have a taster of you for a couple of days a week. I'd end up living for only that time I spent with you. I want you in my bed every day, and I won't be able to function without you."

The knot in my stomach released. He wasn't going to say this wasn't going to work then? In some ways, perhaps it would be easier if he had, but now I knew we both felt the same way. I didn't want to go days without seeing him either.

"What about if we get you a disguise?" he suggested. "An expensive wig and a pair of glasses?"

I laughed. "A disguise?"

But he wasn't joking. "You can use the staff entrance at the rear of the hotel. It's got a security code, but I'm happy for you to have it. You can come and go as you please and you'll be less likely to be seen. Keep the wig and glasses in your bag and slip them on when you come to East London. No one will recognise you."

I covered my face with my hand. "This is insane. You know that, right?"

"What can I say? I'm crazy about you. Maybe that's made me a little insane."

I suspected there was a good dose of craziness inside him well before I came along, but for some reason that only added to his appeal.

He grinned at me. "Now, what kind of wig do you want?"

I couldn't resist him.

"Ooh, something completely different to what I have now." I lifted a clump of my long, blonde curls. "A dark, jaw-length bob, maybe, so I can strut around like a sexy businesswoman in my new glasses."

He caught me by the waist and ducked his head to nibble my neck. "That would look so hot on you."

I ground up against him. "Yeah, you think? You up for a little role playing? The bad boy seduces the uptight business lady?"

"Bad boy, huh?" he growled against my ear. "Is that what you think I am?"

"You're definitely not good."

He licked the lobe of my ear. "I'm good at plenty of things."

How did he always do this to me? Whenever I was with him, all I wanted was to tear off his clothes and lose myself in his body. He was a drug, and I was completely addicted.

But we were also in public, and I was still fearful of someone seeing us. I wished I was someone who could give in to what they wanted without worrying about the consequences, but when the consequences were as severe as they might be in this case, it wasn't just a matter of throwing caution to the wind.

I forced myself from his arms. "I have to go, Jay. I mean it this time."

I glanced left and right, just to make sure we hadn't caught the attention of anyone else. No one seemed to be looking, but that didn't mean there weren't eyes secreted somewhere. I thought of when he'd come to the pub that time, and the number of people who'd seen us together then.

I really was playing with fire.

"You're killing me, Ivy," he said, but he let me go. "I'll have those items couriered to you later so you can come to the hotel."

I still wasn't sure it was a good idea, but I also couldn't stand the thought of living without him.

Chapter Eleven
Jayden

I hated that the fucking Gilligans were putting pressure on Ivy. I understood why they wouldn't want her to see me—if I had a daughter, I wouldn't want her dating someone like me either—but at the same time, it still made me furious. She was an adult, and she should be the one to get to decide who she spent time with. I didn't want them controlling her life.

It bothered me that she'd even considered us not seeing each other. Did that mean I was in this a hell of a lot deeper than she was? I wanted her to not care about what her family thought, and we'd just deal with the consequences.

She was mine. I wanted her to myself. I wanted to be the one to own her.

I knew now that she was who I wanted to be with, no doubts in my mind. Together, we would be a power couple, like Tam and Hallie, and, one day, I'd put a baby in her belly, and we'd become our own family—fuck the others. We didn't need anyone else if we had each other. What the fuck could the Gilligans do about it? Would they attempt to hurt their own sister and daughter? If they came after me, they'd have the Cornells to deal with as well. I didn't know them well, but I didn't think they were that stupid.

If the Gilligans made her choose between me and them, I was determined to make sure they lost. Ivy just needed to come round to my way of thinking.

I arranged for a discreet courier to take over the items I'd promised her.

I had work I needed to concentrate on—including a meeting with Tam and a potential supplier, one I thought would be able to undercut anyone the Gilligans might be working with. Maybe it was against the rules to try to encroach on their territory, but now more than ever I wanted the Gilligans out of this fucking city. I still blamed them for my father's death, and they were most likely responsible for killing Harvey Cornell on his wedding day, too. They were a poison in this city, and they needed to be gone.

My new plan was that they'd leave Ivy behind. With me.

How would Ivy feel about that? Did it even matter? She couldn't possibly want to stay with a family who tried to control her like that.

Before Ivy came over, I had work to do.

I left to meet with Tam. The alliance between our two families now meant that anything to do with business had to be signed off on both sides. I preferred to do things myself. If Tam tried to overrule me on this, I'd be seriously pissed off, but I doubted he would. It made good business sense. A lower price meant we'd make more money off our current customers and could offer a better deal to anyone new we were bringing on board, such as people who were currently working with the Gilligans.

I walked into the Indian restaurant on Brick Lane but didn't wait to be asked to be seated. Instead, I ignored everyone and crossed through to the back of the building, through the busy kitchen, the aroma of spices assaulting my senses, and out into a private dining room at the rear. Tam was already there, a drink on the table in front of him, and he got to his feet and shook my hand.

I took a seat across from him. A waitress hurried over, and I ordered.

"I'll take whatever he's having."

As much as he pissed me off, Tam had good taste.

I checked my watch. We were both early, which was a good thing.

"Any news on the name I gave you?" I asked. I still hadn't forgotten about my mission to track down whoever Doyle was.

Something crossed his face.

I leaned forwards. "You know something, don't you?"

"I'm not sure yet. I want to keep digging before I say anything. It's not heading in the direction either of us thought."

"Spill it," I said.

"Not yet. I know what you're like. You're still too impulsive, and I don't want a trail of bodies left behind if I'm wrong."

I considered arguing with him for a moment, then decided against it. Once Tam had made his mind up about something, it was near impossible to get him to change it. As long as he told me what he found out in the end, it would amount to the same thing. The thought surprised me. Since when had I learned patience? Or was it simply that I was distracted with Ivy?

I changed the subject. "How's Hallie feeling?"

Tam twisted his lips. "She's been having some twinges."

"Does that mean the baby will come soon?" I knew absolutely nothing about labour except that it sounded painful and messy.

"It should. She's due any day now." He nodded down at his phone on the table. "That's why I have to keep that near."

I sat back and folded my arms. "How are you feeling about impending fatherhood?"

Tam smiled—an expression that didn't normally appear on his features. "I can't wait. Seeing that baby in Hallie's arms will be the best moment of my life."

Was I jealous of him? Yeah, maybe a bit. It all seemed so easy between the two of them, but it hadn't always been that way. I should know—I was one of the people who'd made things harder. I regretted that now. But Hallie hadn't acted as though she'd ever wanted to marry Tam—at least not at first—and I'd thought I was doing her a favour. Things had worked out between the two of them.

Tam took a sip of his drink. "What about you? Anyone on the scene?"

There was no way I was going to tell him about Ivy. I could imagine his reaction if I told him I was fucking her. He'd say I was mixing business with pleasure and that it would only lead to disaster. He was probably right, but I had no intention of stopping.

I grinned and lied blatantly to his face. "Yeah, lots of people on the scene. Don't you miss it? A different pussy every night?"

Tam shook his head. "Nah, not for one second. All those girls who only saw the money and the name. Hallie gets me. We're equals. I wouldn't swap her for a thousand of those girls."

A few months ago, I'd probably have laughed at him. How could having one pussy forever possibly be better than tasting a different one every night? But now I got it. I had zero interest in anyone else. All I wanted was Ivy, and I thought she felt the same way.

The possibility of Ivy so much as looking at another man filled me with instant rage. She was mine. If I thought she'd even glanced in the direction of someone else, I'd rip both his arms from his body.

Movement came in the doorway, and Tam and I exchanged a glance. Two suited men walked into the room, and we both rose to shake their hands.

Our meeting had started.

***

A couple of hours later, I was back in the penthouse of my hotel. The meeting had gone smoothly. The men all wanted to expand their business, so the deal worked well for everyone—well, everyone except the Gilligans, of course.

I felt a twinge of guilt that I was conspiring to run Ivy's family out of the city behind her back. Should I tell her? No, that wouldn't do anyone any good, and Tam would fucking kill me.

It wasn't that I didn't trust her. I just didn't want to put her in a difficult position. Besides, she knew how our families worked.

I wanted to hear her say fuck them. Fuck her family. I wanted her to say she didn't give a shit what they thought and that all we needed was each other. But in our world, you didn't just get to say 'fuck 'em'. In our world, upsetting the wrong people—even if that meant family, or maybe *especially* if that meant family—could get someone seriously hurt or even killed.

My thoughts went to Tam and Hallie and the baby they were expecting. That was how it should be. That was what I wanted with Ivy. I'd hinted at it with her before, but she hadn't taken me seriously. Maybe I needed to try harder.

The lift pinged to signal someone was using it.

A moment later, the doors opened, and Ivy stepped out wearing the short dark bob and black framed glasses I'd bought her. It really was a good disguise. I doubted even I'd have recognised her if I'd passed her on the street, though she definitely would have caught my attention.

"Holy shit," I said, aware I was gawping at her. "You look incredible."

She smiled flirtatiously and tucked the hair behind her ear. "You like?"

I did, but I also wanted her to be herself.

"I do, but I missed you."

I slipped the glasses from her face and removed the wig, then undid her hair. Her blonde waves fell down her back.

"Better," I said.

A day without seeing her felt like months.

We didn't even speak; we just crashed together, our mouths finding each other's, tearing at our clothes. We stumbled together into the bedroom and within minutes, I had her in just her knickers on my bed. I covered her with my body and feasted on her skin, kissing, licking, nibbling her lips, her jaw, her breasts, down to her flat stomach.

There, I paused, and lifted my head again.

"If I put a baby in your belly, no one will be able to tear us apart. We'll be like Hallie and Tam—one unit."

She stared into my eyes.

"We're too young, Jay."

"What the fuck does age matter? It's not like either of us are short of money. I have a place for us to live. I want you. I want to be with you. I want to watch your belly swell and grow and know that there's a part of me inside you."

"You know that's not going to work for us."

"I don't know that." I slipped my hand down the inside of her thigh. "We'd have a lot of fun trying."

She shoved at my shoulder. "Jay, stop it."

I dipped my tongue into her navel, tasting her skin. "I'd tie you to the bed and fill your sweet pussy with my cum, over and over, until it's dripping out of you and you're swollen with it."

I knew she liked the way I spoke to her.

She let out a groan, and her thighs parted, giving me easier access.

"You'd be so perfect, Ivy. I'd keep your legs spread so I could see my cum dripping out of you. You'd take it so well. I know you would."

A breathy sigh escaped her, and she relaxed against me. I grazed my fingers up her silky soft skin, to the juncture of her thighs, and then across the gusset of her underwear. The material was already damp, and she rolled her hips, pressing onto my hand. She was always so hungry for it. It was one of the things I loved about her.

"What about after I got pregnant?" she said, buying into the fantasy now. "Would you still want to fuck me?"

"Hell, yes. I could fuck you even more then because I wouldn't need to worry about getting you pregnant."

She giggled. "That doesn't make sense."

I loved her laugh, especially if I was the one to cause the sound. "Any excuse," I told her.

I moved up her body and kissed her mouth again, then feathered those kisses across her cheek and jaw.

"Let me come inside you," I murmured against her ear. "I want to feel your pussy around my cock. I want to ride you bare, and if you get pregnant, we'll both be happy about it, I know we will."

She groaned. "My family—"

"They'd have to find out about us, and they'd have to accept it."

I yanked her underwear to one side and slipped a finger inside her and rubbed her clit with my thumb. She was so beautifully wet.

I didn't want to be bound to the Gilligans, but this wouldn't be an alliance in the same way Hallie and Tam's marriage had bound the Wynters and Cornells. My plan was to weaken the Gilligans. I'd take Ivy from them, and, with some of the new deals I had in place, I'd start to encroach on the Gilligan territory. Having Ivy at my side would strengthen my position.

"My studies," she protested, squirming beneath me. "I graduate this year. I've got my exams."

I plunged my fingers in and out of her, just the way she liked it.

"You won't get pregnant right away. We'll just have months of trying, and by the time you do get pregnant, you'll have graduated before you have the baby. And if it happens before, we'll get you extra help, whatever you need. It's not like I can't afford everything and anything you could ever want."

She drew in a breath, her lips parting with pleasure. "Okay, do it."

"Are you sure?"

"Yes, do it. I want to feel you, too."

I eased her knickers down her thighs and threw them to one side. My cock was already rock-hard and growing harder by the second at the anticipation of taking her bare.

I positioned my erection at her pussy.

"Slowly," she said. "I want to watch every inch of you sink into me."

The heat of her warmed the smooth head of my dick, and I used my hold on it to rub back and forth, dipping inside for a second before moving up to her clit and back down again.

"Oh, that feels good," she groaned.

"Your pussy is so pretty for me, baby. God, it's like you were made to take my cock."

"Yes, I want it. Fill me up."

She arched her back, begging for it.

I edged inside her another inch. I was so hard, I felt like I was impaling her. I used my thumb on her clit, rubbing firm circles.

She let out a whimper. "More, give me more."

I nudged my hips forwards, giving her what she wanted and sank right down to the hilt. I held her firm, not letting her move, and holding still myself, just wanting to bask in the sensation of her tight pussy surrounding my bare dick.

"Fuck, Ivy. I'm going to fuck you and fill you with my cum."

Her pussy walls pulsed around me.

She tilted her head back and moaned. I pushed my thumb into her mouth, and she sucked on it like it was my cock. Fuck. Was it possible to get turned on any more?

"You turn me on so much. You're so right for me, Ivy. I don't want anyone else, ever. Do you understand me."

She nodded, my thumb still in her mouth, my dick in her cunt.

"Look at me," I commanded. "Look in my fucking eyes. You're the one for me. There's no one else in this world."

I didn't care that she was from the wrong family. I meant what I'd said. I'd been screwing around for years, and no girl I'd ever been with affected me the way she did. Was it because she understood me, that we came from similar backgrounds? I had no idea. She was beautiful, and smart, and strong.

She rocked her hips, urging me on. I couldn't hold still any longer. As much as I didn't want this to end, the need to come was taking over everything else. I drew back, my eyes still fixed on her cunt and the way she stretched around my girth. I paused before I slipped from her completely and shoved back in. Ivy cried out.

I started up a rhythm. I ducked my head to her tits and sucked her nipples, tweaking them, hard enough to hurt, just how she liked it. She reached out and clawed her nails into my back and arse, leaving marks on me like her very own branding.

"Make those noises for me," I told her. "I love to hear you. Your cries are so fucking sexy."

She whimpered and thrashed her head from side to side. Her whole body was a taut string, ready to snap. I kept up my attention on her clit, rubbing the swollen nub faster as I fucked her.

Heat gathered in my cock, and I knew I wasn't going to last much longer. My hips pistoned, slamming into her, over and over.

"Oh fuck, Jay. Do it. Come inside me. I want to feel you."

Her pussy clenched and released around me. Her cries grew higher and faster, and I could tell she was close.

"Now," she breathed. "Now."

She unravelled underneath me, shaking and shuddering, and I emptied inside her with a groan, releasing all the air from my lungs. I dropped down, pressing my forehead to hers as we inhaled each other's breath. The orgasm shuddered through me in a little aftershock, my cock twitching inside her, releasing hot stream after stream. She still felt so good, my dick bathed in my semen and her juices.

I kissed her mouth. "You took me so beautifully, baby girl. You did so well. I want to stay inside you forever."

She sank into the mattress. "That felt incredible."

I kissed the tip of her nose. "I'm already looking forward to doing that to you all over again."

I grew soft inside her and slipped from her body. I rose to my knees between her legs and caught her by the ankles.

Ivy squealed and kicked out at me. "What are you doing?"

Holding her firm, I spun her around and hooked her heels over the top of the headboard.

"Jay," she protested. "I look ridiculous."

I planted a kiss to her bare sole. "You're sexy as fuck. Spread those legs for me a bit more."

She bit her lower lip, suddenly coy.

"Do it," I demanded.

She did, allowing me a perfect view of her cunt. The milky white of my cum glistened between her pussy lips, and I shifted my position slightly to give myself better access. I dipped my fingers into her slit, pushing the cum back inside her pussy.

"Don't want any of it escaping."

"Jay—" she groaned, but it was only half a protest.

"If I make you orgasm again, will that pull the cum even higher up inside you?" I wondered out loud.

She pouted. "I don't know. You could try."

She was so wet, dribbling down over her asshole. I pushed just the tip of my finger inside her tight star.

"Oh," she gasped. "I didn't think—"

But her words cut off as I worked my finger right into her hole. With my other hand, I placed it low on her belly and used my fingers to work her clit, while I fingered her arse. With my thumb, I blocked her pussy, preventing any more of my cum from sliding out of her.

Within seconds, I had her squirming and mewling, her head thrown back, her eyes closed. Her breasts were flushed with heat, and they jiggled every time I pushed my finger inside her arse.

Her back arched from the bed, and she cursed, her fingers digging into the sheets on either side. I loved how she responded to me, and I pictured myself fucking her again, filling her with my seed over and over.

Chapter Twelve

Ivy

I shook and trembled as I came hard for the second time, my body convulsing around his fingers.

I slumped back on the mattress, though my legs were still in the air. I shoved my sweaty hair out of my face. "Jesus Christ."

He chuckled. "You can just call me Jay."

I smirked at him, and he kissed me, then got off the bed to use the bathroom.

I closed my eyes, suddenly exhausted. I didn't bother trying to take my legs down again, he wouldn't allow it. Could we have actually done enough to create a baby? I didn't think so. My period was due any day now, and I was pretty sure I needed to be in the middle of my cycle to get pregnant. I didn't want to ruin things for Jay, though, and anyway, I liked how he treated me, like I was someone special. If he treated me this way now, what would he be like when I was carrying his baby? He'd worship the ground I walked on, and I craved his attention and approval like it was a drug.

I knew he was crazy, but maybe, so was I? How could I not be after growing up in my family?

I pictured us living somewhere—not in the penthouse apartment, but an actual house, maybe even somewhere outside of London. I imagined us having land attached with stables, so our children could have ponies and learn to ride.

Maybe I'd get some chickens and a dog, and we could forget all about city life and just enjoy each other and our own family.

My father and brothers were going to have to find out about us eventually, but Jay was right. If I got pregnant with his child, there wouldn't be a single thing they could do about separating us. Even so, the thought of breaking the news to them churned my stomach. They'd be furious. What if they tried to send me away? Jayden would never allow it, but the thought of that conflict between him and my family terrified me.

My family loved me in their own, strange way. I just had to hope that love was stronger than the hate they had for Jayden Wynter. Ultimately, they'd want me to be happy, wouldn't they?

Jay returned to the bed.

I twisted towards him. "You know you're not the only one who's going to need to use the bathroom. I'm going to have to move eventually."

He laughed. "Okay, I'm not going to hold you hostage. Shall I order some food in?"

My heart sank. "I can't stay. My family are going to be watching my every move right now. I'm going to need to swing by the library on my way home so I can justify where I've been."

His face fell. "Fuck. I wish you could stay here all night. I want to be able to wake up with you in my arms."

"I want that, too, but I need to go."

I thought he was going to give me an argument, but he didn't. "Okay. Is there anything I can do? I can call you a taxi?"

"No, I'm fine. I'll just use the bathroom and get dressed, then I'll make my way back to North London."

I got up from the bed and his cum slid down the inside of my legs. He caught me in a bearhug, pressing his nose to my hair.

"Jay," I protested. "I'm going to make a mess of your carpet."

"I don't care. I wish you could stay."

"I wish the same, but I can't."

And he let me go.

***

I left Jay's hotel and caught the Tube to my university campus. It was harder for someone to keep track of me if I used public transport. I'd worn the disguise while leaving the hotel, but as soon as no one else was around, I whipped it off again and stuffed it back in my bag. I didn't want anyone asking why I was wearing it.

After a brief stint at the library, I went back to my house.

My eldest brother, Bruno, was already there, waiting for me.

I threw my keys down and sighed. "Is this how it's going to be now? Will I always have someone here making sure I get home on time?"

He checked his watch. "Is this on time? Where have you been?"

"At the library. Just like I always am."

Bruno snorted. "You really expect me to believe that. I know you can be a bit of a nerd, but you're not that much of a loser."

"I'm not a nerd or a loser!"

"Always got your head in a book."

"I know how to read," I snapped. "Maybe you should try it sometime. Might expand your brain a bit."

He caught me in a headlock and dug his knuckles into my scalp.

"Bruno!" I protested. "Get off!"

He gave me one final knuckle to my head and then released me. I jerked away from him and straightened, shoving my hair back.

I hoped I'd managed to distract Bruno, but he was his typical dog with a bone.

"You know I'll be able to contact the library to see if you did check in when you said you did."

I shrugged as though it was no big deal. "I didn't sign in. The gate was open, so I just walked through. And stop acting like such a stalker. It's not my fault if there's someone out there who looks like me. This is London, after all. There's over nine million people who live here. I'm pretty sure there's bound to be at least one other five-feet-one, blonde girl wandering around."

He studied my face as though he was trying to read my lie in my eyes. I hated being untruthful to him. I'd never lied directly to my family before all this—at least never about anything important. But there was no way I could ever let them know I'd been at Jayden's hotel, and they'd go nuts if they thought there had been something physical between us.

"Go home, Bruno. There's nothing to see here. My life is as dull as dishwater. I'm sure you have better places to be."

He laughed. "Yeah, I have plenty of better places to be, but that doesn't mean we don't have eyes on you, Ivy. You're acting differently, and everyone has noticed. Maybe we don't know exactly what's going on with you, but we will."

"You can stalk me all you like," I repeated, "but you're wasting your time. Now, I'm going to bed."

"Fine. Goodnight, Ivy."

I didn't bother saying goodnight to him, but ice settled in my heart as I climbed the stairs to bed. I had the feeling I was going to need something far better than a stupid wig and a pair of glasses if I was going to keep this a secret.

I reached my room, and in a sudden panic, hid everything I had that could be linked back to Jay. As much as I didn't want to delete all his messages, I made myself do it, and I changed his contact number to 'Prof T'. Worried one of my family members might come in and search my bag, I also hid the disguise and his key down the back of my chest of drawers.

Would it be enough? I couldn't shake the feeling that it wouldn't be.

They were going to find out, no matter what I did.

Chapter Thirteen

Jayden

I burst into the hospital and rushed up to the desk.

"Hallie Wynter," I blurted to the nurse sitting behind it. I realised my mistake. "I mean Cornell. Hallie Cornell. What room is she in?"

It was three in the morning when I'd received the call from Tam saying Hallie had gone into labour, but things hadn't gone to plan.

"Take a right down there," she said. "Room three-oh-five."

My shoes squeaked on the flooring as I ran towards the room.

Tam stood in the corridor outside with his hand covering his mouth. My breath lodged in a ball in my throat. Fuck, no. Please let Hallie be okay. I couldn't stand the thought of losing my sister.

"Tam?" I practically shouted. "Tam, how is she? How's my sister? Is she alive?"

"Yes, she's alive. She's not good, though."

I exhaled for what felt like the first time since I'd got the call. "Oh, thank fuck. I want to see her."

"Not now. She's not even woken up yet."

"She almost died, Tam. I want to see her."

He positioned himself in front of the hospital room doors. "No, she shouldn't be disturbed."

I shoved him in the chest. "Get out my fucking way."

"Don't fucking touch me."

"What is all this?" one of the nurses snapped at us. "You want to brawl, go to a bar. This is a hospital. It's not even visiting hours."

I assumed Tam had thrown some extra money around to make sure he got to stay.

We both took a breath, and Tam stepped out of the way.

I looked in at the private hospital room.

Hallie seemed somehow shrunken—and I didn't just mean her belly. Her cheeks were gaunt, her colouring sallow. How could twenty-four hours have changed a person so much? Around her, machines beeped steadily, and a drip was threaded into the back of her hand.

My chest tightened. "Hallie?"

She was unconscious and couldn't hear me, but I still wanted her attention. Fuck, I was a selfish son of a bitch. She was my big sister and had practically raised me, and here she was, having gone through a trauma, and all I wanted was for her to wake up and make me feel better.

I turned back to Tam, who'd followed me in.

"Where's the baby?" I asked.

Tam covered his face with his hands. "She's in the Neonatal Intensive Care. She wasn't breathing for a little while after she was born. She had the cord wrapped around her neck and then she got stuck, but the doctors and midwives were brilliant. They got her breathing again, but they want to keep an eye on her."

"And Hallie?"

"She lost a lot of blood. She's had to have a transfusion."

"Jesus. We could have lost them both."

"*I* could have lost them both. She's my wife, and that's my baby."

"And she's my sister and my niece. It's not a fucking competition, Tam. We're both allowed to love her."

I realised he was scared. Not just scared, fucking terrified. Tam Cornell had finally come across a situation where he hadn't been able to control the outcome, and it had rocked him to the core. These were the people he loved most in the world—the people who'd become his family outside of the other Cornells—and if he'd lost Hallie and the baby it would have destroyed him.

"Has she got a name yet? The baby, I mean."

"No. We talked about a couple, but Hallie said she wanted to meet her first. I thought it would happen right after the baby was born, that the midwife would put her in Hallie's arms and we'd decide what her name would be together, but it didn't happen that way." His voice grew thick as he spoke.

Tam was close to tears. The man who practically ran most of London had been reduced to a mess because of the love he had for his wife and baby.

"Hey, it's going to be okay. These things never end up the same way we picture them, but as long as they're both going to be all right, that's all that matters."

Tam's lips pinched, and he turned his head, clearly embarrassed about his emotion.

"Did you get hold of Layla?" I asked. "Hallie would want her best friend here for support."

Tam shook his head. "I tried, but she's away with her family. She won't be back for a few days."

"What about Leo? Is he coming in with Kaja?"

I thought Tam could probably do with the support of his brother rather than it being me.

Tam blew the air out of his lungs. "Yeah, they'll come in the morning. They wanted to let things settle down before we start crowding Hallie. She's going to be feeling pretty rough and probably frightened, too, when she wakes."

"She needs to know the baby is alive the second she wakes up. She won't know what happened and all she'll realise is that she's not pregnant anymore, and she'll want to know what's happened to her baby."

He blinked back tears. "She doesn't even know it's a baby girl. I tried to tell her, but I don't think she was really conscious."

It felt strange to have someone like Tam leaning on me. One minute, he'd been ready to throw me out, the next I'd been practically handing him a tissue. I envied him, though. He knew exactly what he wanted and wasn't afraid to tell Hallie either. I wanted what he had, even with the pain and fear of loss.

A family of my own.

Chapter Fourteen

Ivy

I'd called Jayden and messaged him but hadn't heard anything. That was unusual. He was normally the one who messaged me first thing, telling me he missed me and wanting to know when he'd get to see me again.

Worry wound through me. Was he okay? I couldn't hide from the fact that he was in a dangerous business, but it wasn't something we talked about. We were from opposite sides of the street, and truth be told, I didn't want to know. I'd never want to be accused of leaking information he'd told me back to my family, and I wouldn't want to hear something that would put me in the middle either.

It was another thing I didn't want to think about.

I forced myself to go into uni and attended my lectures. I tried to concentrate on what my professors were saying, but I kept checking my phone, hoping for a message to come through. Minutes ticked by into hours, and my stomach knotted tighter and tighter.

There was no one I could call to check that he was okay. If I did, people would instantly start asking questions. Jay and I weren't supposed to even really know each other outside of knowing that we existed. If I contacted anyone at all to ask about him, they'd want to know why I was interested.

I had no choice but to be patient and hope he got in touch soon. I also kept an eye on the local news for any reports of shooting or violence in the city. Unfortunately, this was London, and violence was a common occurrence.

I dragged myself through the day.

After another lecture had finished, Kyle caught up with me. We'd barely spoken since that night at the pub, and, to be honest, that had been perfectly fine with me.

"What's got your goat?" he asked.

"Sorry?"

"You look miserable. Is that arsehole from the pub giving you problems?"

"That's none of your business, Kyle."

"He is, isn't he? Got more muscle than brains. You can't trust men like that, Ivy."

What did he know? My entire family was like that. But they were criminals, and I couldn't get away from that fact. Could Jay have met someone else? My heart wrenched at the possibility. No, I didn't believe it of him. The way we were together wasn't just in my head. He felt the same way about me, I was sure of it. We had something special.

Maybe my father and brothers did break the law, but they were loyal, weren't they? That was the one thing I'd always been able to depend upon—them being loyal to our family. Now I was the one betraying that loyalty. I couldn't even bring myself to think about how my family would react if they found out I was sleeping with Jayden Wynter. And it wasn't as though we were just sleeping together either, was it? He'd been the only one to mention the word love, but the intensity we had together couldn't be just a crush. I'd never been in love before, and while it wasn't a question I'd ever asked him, I knew he'd never been in a serious relationship before we'd met. All he'd ever done was screw around.

Maybe he'd got bored of being with only one girl and he'd decided to go back to being a player? Could it have all just been fake—the way he looked into my eyes, the things he said to me, the way he touched me? Could it all have been an act?

No, I didn't believe it.

My phone buzzed, the sound continuing, telling me it was a call rather than a message. My heart leapt, and I snatched it up. The name Prof T was on the screen.

I turned my back on Kyle, and heard his footsteps as he walked off, no doubt shaking his head at me.

"Jay? Are you okay?"

To my relief, his now familiar voice replied. "Yeah, I'm fine."

I didn't know what I'd been expecting but until I'd actually heard his voice for myself, I was still worried that someone had his phone and might have been calling to deliver bad news.

"Oh my God, Jay, I've been so worried about you."

He sounded tired. "I'm fine. It's Hallie. She had her baby."

"That's wonderful news." Why didn't he seem happier?

"The birth didn't go well."

My stomach knotted. "Is everyone okay?"

"Hallie hasn't woken up yet. She haemorrhaged and lost a lot of blood."

I sat down heavily. "Oh no. That's awful. Will she be all right?"

"We don't know yet. We won't know until she wakes up. "

"What about the baby?"

"She took a little while to start breathing after the birth, but they think she's going to be okay."

"It's a little girl?" I checked.

"Yes."

"How lovely. They have a daughter."

Despite what Hallie had gone through—and was still going through—I couldn't help the stab of jealousy that got me in the heart. I pictured how it would be to have a family you'd both chosen and created. A reason for living for someone other than myself.

"When can I see you?" I asked, missing him terribly.

"Tam is beside himself. I can't leave them."

"No, of course not. I understand." My heart ached. "I wish I could be there for you."

"I wish you could be here, too. There's nothing I wouldn't give right now to feel your arms around me."

I pictured myself holding him, of him burying his face in my neck, taking comfort in me. We sat in silence on the phone, and it felt like our hearts were speaking, even if we couldn't be together physically.

"This is so shit," I whispered. "I wish things were different."

"Me too."

"Sorry, you've got bigger things to worry about."

"It's okay. I'm going to be dealing with things here for the next few days, and all the family is around. I won't be able to get away without someone noticing."

I understood what he was saying—we wouldn't be able to see each other without someone seeing us.

I wished I could bring Hallie and the baby a gift. Do what a normal girlfriend would do when their boyfriend had become an uncle and there was a new baby in the family. Instead, I felt like a complete outcast. It was selfish of me to even be thinking this way. Poor Hallie was really sick and hadn't even got to meet her new baby yet. That was far more important than my stupid relationship woes. That knowledge still didn't stop me having them, though. In that moment, I hated my last name and everything that came with it. I wanted to be someone different.

Did I really think I could walk away from being a Gilligan?

My father and brothers would never allow it, and I didn't even know if I'd be welcomed in the Cornell and Wynter clan. Then I remembered the story behind how Leo Cornell and Kaja Valk got together, how her father had killed Leo's fiancée, and I wondered if perhaps I had a chance. If they'd accepted Kaja into the family, maybe they'd accept me, too.

Jay's voice came down the line. "I'd better go, baby. I'll stay in touch, okay?"

We ended the call, and I sat with the phone in my hand. A tear slipped down my cheek, and I wiped it away. I wasn't even totally sure what I was crying about. Was it that I felt excluded? Was it because I missed him? Was it for Hallie and her baby girl?

I toyed with the idea of buying that present for Hallie and the baby and just showing up at the hospital, but I knew I couldn't. The last thing the Cornells needed right now was me throwing a bomb into the middle of everything. It would be a purely selfish move.

Plus, then I'd have to deal with the fallout, and it wouldn't be pretty. My family would find out I was messing around with a Wynter, and I didn't even want to think about what their reaction would be. They would be furious, and when people like my father and brothers got furious, people got hurt.

Chapter Fifteen
Jayden

It had been a hard day.

Tam and I alternated sitting beside Hallie's bed and sitting at the plastic cot next to the baby, neither of us wanting to leave either of them alone.

I was jealous of them. It was fucking stupid, but I was. Jealous of Tam and Hallie—even though Hallie was unconscious—and jealous of Leo and Kaja for getting to be together, despite what her father had done. They'd been keeping us supplied with coffee and food and general moral support.

I wanted nothing more than to have Ivy here with me. It felt so fucking wrong that she wasn't. She should be here.

It scared me shitless just how hard I'd fallen for her. I'd never experienced intense feelings like this in my life. She'd completely taken over my head and my heart. Girls had always been fun before, but that was all. The moment they'd made noises about wanting me around, I'd run for the hills. But now, I felt like the one making the noises. Did Ivy feel the same way? I thought she did. Though she'd never said she loved me out loud, just the way we were together, constantly needing to be touching, even just the way we smiled at each other, as though we had a secret from the rest of the world, told me this was more than just a fling.

Tam entered the hospital room where I'd been watching over Hallie while he sat with the baby. We'd swap over, so he got to spend some time with his wife. Whether Hallie knew we were there or not, I had no idea.

"How's she doing?" Tam asked.

I shook my head. "No change."

He dragged his hand through his hair. "Fuck."

Tam was normally well put together, but right now, he looked a wreck. Pale skin with dark smudges beneath his eyes, his hair all over the place. His shirt open at the neck and untucked, his suit jacket a crumpled ball on the chair, his sleeves pushed up to his elbows.

"What about the baby?" I asked.

"She's stable. I feel like she should have a name, but I can't decide on one without Hallie's input. She'd fucking kill me."

We both looked to the woman lying in the hospital bed. It had only been a matter of hours, but what if she didn't wake up? What if days and weeks went by and the baby girl still didn't have a name? I suddenly saw the danger in that. Would naming her be like giving up—like admitting Hallie wouldn't ever wake?

I put my hand on Tam's shoulder and gave it a squeeze and then left him to go down to the neonatal unit. It was on the same floor, ensuring that the mothers and babies were never too far apart.

There were already several parents sitting with their babies. One mother and father sat beside a tiny set of twins. In comparison, Hallie's baby was huge, and I almost felt the need to explain to the others the reason for her being here.

I took a seat beside the baby's cot. She was sleeping, and I studied her tiny, wrinkled face, trying to figure out who she looked like. A little knitted hat was pulled down over her head, so I couldn't even see what colour hair she had. I was sure someone else might be able to work it out, but she just looked like a newborn baby to me.

I became aware of one of the nurses standing beside me.

"You can hold her, if you want?" she said.

I shook my head. "Oh, no. That's probably not a good idea."

"Yes, it is. It's important baby gets some skin-to-skin contact."

"I'm not her father," I explained. "I'm her uncle."

"I'm sure she won't mind."

I realised what skin-to-skin meant. "You want me to take my shirt off?"

She gave me a wink. "I absolutely do."

I grinned. She was old enough to be my mother—possibly even grandmother—but that didn't seem to bother her. It felt good to have someone a bit light-hearted around after all the trauma.

She continued. "It's been proven that babies who get skin-to-skin contact have lower stress levels and cry less than those who don't. They can regulate their breathing and body temperate better, too, among a whole host of other things."

"I've never held a baby before."

It felt like a stupid thing to admit to. I was completely out of my depth, taking care of a baby, and I didn't like being out of my depth. Lack of control was something I railed against, and it seemed ridiculous to be shaken up over someone who didn't even weigh ten pounds.

"Don't worry. I won't tell her."

She scooped the baby girl out of the plastic incubator. She still had little monitors stuck to her skin, and she seemed ridiculously tiny.

Fuck.

I stripped off my shirt, leaving me bare-chested, and sat in the comfortable chair that I assumed was here for nursing mothers or for fathers to do this exact thing.

The nurse handed her to me, and I cradled her to my chest. Her little face nuzzled my skin, her mouth opening and closing. She didn't wake, though.

"Hello, little one. I'm your uncle, Jayden."

I wished Ivy was here to see this. What would she think?

To my surprise, I found myself relaxing with the baby. Poor Hallie, missing out on her daughter's first hours. She was going to hate that she wasn't awake for this.

"I'm sorry your mummy hasn't been able to hold you yet," I told the baby. "But she will soon. Very soon."

I hoped I was right.

***

The time came to swap over again. I went to relieve Tam.

"How's the baby?" he asked.

"Good. I held her while she slept. She's really cute. I wish Hallie was awake to meet her."

We both turned to my sister's bed.

Hallie's eyes fluttered open.

Tam was there in an instant, taking her hand. "Hallie? It's okay, sweetheart. I'm here."

"Tam?" she said. "What happened?"

Then her memory must have come back to her as her eyes widened and she reached to her belly. "The baby? Oh God. Where's my baby?"

She tried to sit up.

"She's fine," Tam said. "The baby is fine. She's just in the NICU for observations. She had a little trouble breathing at first, but she's healthy."

Hallie fell back against the bed. "Thank God."

"You were the one we've all been worried about," he said. "You gave us hell of a scare."

"What happened?"

"You haemorrhaged. Something about the blood vessels where the placenta was attached not clotting. I don't know any more details than that, but you've been given a lot of blood." He nodded to the drips still feeding into her veins.

"I want to see my baby. Did you say it's a girl?"

He smiled. "Yes, a baby girl. Seven pounds five ounces, with a head of curly black hair."

She returned the smile. "Lots of hair? That'll explain all the heartburn then. I'm blaming that on you."

He laughed and squeezed her hand. "I'm just glad you're okay. I couldn't have done this on my own, Hallie. You know that, don't you. I don't work without you anymore, and I sure as hell wouldn't have a clue about how to take care of a newborn baby."

"That makes two of us then."

Tam glanced over his shoulder at me. "Jayden's here, too. He's been helping to look after the baby."

Hallie smiled, though it was tired. "Jayden with a baby? Never."

I grinned at my sister. "I guess I've surprised you."

Knowing they needed some private family time, I left them to it, texting Ivy as I walked out of the hospital.

I need to see you. Meet me at my place? ASAP?

Her reply came almost instantly. *See you there.*

A smile touched my lips.

We arrived at the penthouse at almost exactly the same time.

"How is every—?"

I didn't give her the chance to finish her sentence, claiming her mouth with mine and swallowing her words. I yanked at her clothes, needing for her to be naked. The fear of what might have happened to my sister and her newborn child turned to lust inside me. I wanted to forget about how I'd felt upon learning she'd haemorrhaged and wasn't waking up.

"Jay," she gasped.

"I need you. I missed you."

"I missed you, too."

We'd only been apart for a day, but it had already been too long. How was I supposed to live without her? The scent of her skin was like an addiction–I couldn't get enough.

But we couldn't see each other in secret forever. Either we had to tell our families or we had to go our separate ways. I knew mine wouldn't be overly happy about the situation, but they'd accept it in the end. Ivy's family, however, was a whole different story.

My hand caught the back of her neck, holding her firm while I kissed her.

She pushed her tongue into my mouth.

God, I was already hard for her.

"I'm going to fuck you. No playing nice, got it?"

She nodded obediently, her beautiful aqua eyes wide. I shoved my hand between her thighs and thrust my fingers roughly inside her. She gasped, but I didn't slow down.

I shoved her up against the wall, pinned her hands over her head, and kissed her roughly. We were both breathing hard, filled with urgency.

I picked her up and placed her on the kitchen counter, knocking things out of the way as I did so. I yanked her knickers down her thighs and over her feet and tossed them away. All I wanted was to be buried inside her.

Freeing myself from my jeans, I positioned myself between her thighs. She hooked her legs around my hips and reached for my cock, placing me at her pussy. Just like I'd promised, I wasn't gentle with her. I drove deep inside her, as deep as I could get, and she clung to me, her nails clawing my back.

I grabbed her arse so I could yank her to meet me, using her like a fuck-toy, driving into her harder.

"You're taking me so well," I praised her from between clenched teeth. Her cunt pulsed around me. "God, fuck, yes, just like that, Ivy, baby. Your pussy is so perfect for me."

Her sweet, tight little snatch hugged my cock. She was so hot. Her head tilted back, her perfect throat exposed. I lowered my head to lick her from the base of her throat right up to her jaw, leaving a trail of saliva behind.

"Are you my good girl?" I said. "Are you here to please me?"

"Oh, yes, I'm a good girl. I am, fuck."

"'Cause only good girls get my cum, and then I'm going to take such good care of you, Ivy. You're going to be my princess, got it?"

I reached between us to rub her clit and slammed into her, harder and harder. We kissed in frantic nips and sucks, our tongues meeting and sliding away again. We were both caught in the hard, fast fucking.

"Oh God, Jay. I'm coming, I'm coming."

I exploded, jamming myself deep, coming hard. I spilled myself inside her—neither of us had mentioned condoms—and I loved that she'd wanted my cum. We held each other tight, our faces buried into each other's necks, clinging to one another as though we were both too afraid to let go.

"God, baby, I'm so proud of you for taking all that. You did so good."

Tears pricked her eyes.

I licked the saltiness from the corners of her lids and then dropped a kiss to her mouth.

"I love you, Jay," she said, more tears spilling down her cheeks. "I love you."

"Then why are you crying? That's the best thing I ever heard. You know I love you, too."

"Because this is never going to work. We're doomed, and I don't know how I'm going to live without you."

"Then don't," I told her. "Don't live without me. Let's just go. I don't care where. I'll get my business in order and make sure Hallie and the baby are okay, and then we'll leave. We'll go to Mexico and live on the beach, or Australia, or anywhere far away from here."

She sniffed and nodded. "I don't think there's any other choice."

I looked into her eyes. "There is a choice, and I choose you, Ivy Gilligan. I choose you every single moment of every single day. Got it?"

She smiled and kissed me. "Got it."

Chapter Sixteen

Ivy

I was turning into a proficient liar.

Whenever my family asked where I was going and what was taking up so much of my time, I was always busy with university stuff, and for those I studied with, including my tutors, I had family issues going on.

I knew now wasn't the best time to be so distracted by Jayden. I should have my head down and be focusing on my coursework and exams, but now we'd made the decision to go, my studies felt pointless. Any time that wasn't spent by his side was time wasted. I craved his touch, and not only that, I just wanted to be around him. I felt like a different person, no longer living in the shadow of my family. I'd been chosen by him, and I felt like I'd finally found my place in the world.

I told myself it was important to live in the moment and not worry about the future, but that wasn't in my nature. I was a worrier and a planner, and this relationship was going against everything that came naturally to me.

I was terrified someone was going to see us, but the longer things went on without anyone saying anything, the more relaxed we became. I'd taken to wearing my wig pulled down over my head whenever I went to visit him at the hotel, which was where we were most of the time. I assumed the man he had on the door was well paid, since he used my name when he greeted me now but had kept my daily visits to himself.

Hallie was doing better. She was home with the baby now which meant Jayden was feeling more confident about going.

Soon, the time would come for us to put together our plans to leave.

We'd decided on Australia as being the perfect place. Everyone there spoke English, and maybe one day, when everything died down, I'd be able to resume my studies. The country was big enough for us to vanish. Neither of us wanted to spend the rest of our lives looking over our shoulders.

Every time I spoke to my father and brothers, I felt like they could read my lies on my face, but I did my best to act normally.

The last thing I needed was for them to find out.

Chapter Seventeen
Jayden

I'd been visiting Hallie and the baby for what might be the last time. I felt drenched with guilt that I wasn't telling my sister about my plans to leave, but I couldn't say a word. Once we were out of the country, I'd let her know we were safe, but before then, I couldn't risk anyone stepping in.

The lift doors slid open, and I exited. Immediately, I drew to a halt.

I wasn't alone.

Bruno Gilligan sat on my dark-brown leather sofa, his legs crossed, nursing a bottle of beer that I assumed had come from my fridge.

"Hello, Jayden."

I tensed. "What the fuck are you doing here? How did you get in?"

He didn't answer my question. "I think you and I need to have a little chat, man to man, about the fact you've been fucking my sister."

There was no point in denying it. He clearly knew.

"Ivy isn't doing anything she doesn't want to. She's a grown woman. She can do whatever she wants."

"Now that part you're wrong about. She might be a grown woman, but she's a Gilligan, and she sure as hell isn't allowed to be with a Wynter." He spat my surname as though the taste of it was bitter.

I folded my arms across my chest, trying to appear nonchalant. I didn't want this to escalate, but I knew it easily could. I scanned Bruno's body, trying to pick out the shape of a weapon beneath his expensive suit. Had he come here armed with a gun or a knife? It would surprise me if he hadn't. He'd clearly come here to fight, but I wasn't going to give him one.

"This might not be what you want, but it's what Ivy wants. This isn't just some fling. I'm not just fucking her. I'm in love with her."

His eyes widened, and he burst out laughing. "In love with her? What kind of bullshit is that?"

I shook my head. "I mean it. I love her, and she loves me. Nothing you say or do is going to stop us from being together. I don't give a shit about any of this anymore." I gestured towards the huge windows and the view of the city lights beyond. "You can take my part of the city. It's yours. Ivy and I will go and live somewhere quiet, together."

"You really think Tam Cornell is just going to let you hand your patch over to us?"

He had a point.

This was one of the people who'd plotted to murder my father. I had the perfect opportunity to take my revenge—Bruno had broken into my home, after all—but I discovered I didn't want that. All I wanted was for Ivy to be happy, and this situation right here wasn't going to make her happy.

I remembered all the times she'd been paranoid about her family finding out about us, how I'd brushed off her concerns, telling her we'd deal with it at the time. This was now that time, and the things I said and did in the next few moments were critical.

"Bruno, how do you think the alliance between myself and Tam Cornell started? It was from my sister marrying Tam. It was never what I wanted. I didn't think the Cornells and Wynters should be anything other than enemies. This could be the same. Ivy could act like a bridge between our families."

He was laughing, mocking. "You want to marry Ivy? Jesus fucking Christ. I don't even want you speaking to Ivy, never mind marrying her. What sort of deluded fucking idiot are you?"

I clenched my teeth. I needed to keep my cool, no matter what insults he threw at me. But I could feel the adrenaline rising inside me like lava. I clenched my fists at my sides. I'd never been known for my self-restraint, and I guaranteed this arsehole was betting on me losing my shit.

"I suggest you leave, Bruno. How do you think Ivy's going to react to you being here right now?" I ground out my words.

"I don't give a fuck how she'll react. It's our job to protect her, and the girl has clearly lost her damned mind."

I noticed he'd said 'our job' but he was the only one here. "Where's your brother? What about your father? Do they know you're here?"

I wondered if one of them had warned him off, told him not to stir up trouble, but he'd come anyway. Did the other family members realise that if they fucked with me, it would not only cause problems, businesswise, but it might also drive Ivy farther away. If that was the case, they were clearly more sensible than Bruno.

He cracked his knuckles. "They knew they could leave this up to me. They have more important things to deal with."

I cocked my head to one side. "So you're just like the hired thug, then?"

My instinct was to storm over there, grab him by the throat, and throw him out of a window. I imagined the very satisfying crunch as he hit the pavement far below, and the screams that would follow as people realised what had happened. But, of course, I couldn't do that. This was my hotel, and Bruno Gilligan being found dead on the pavement outside of it would bring about too many questions. I just needed for him to leave. Should I say I wouldn't keep seeing Ivy, just to appease him? It was tempting, if only to bring this situation to a close, but then what would happen? I had no intention of letting Ivy go, so I'd only turn around in another month from now to find him or the other brother, Aiden, back on my sofa.

I wanted a life with Ivy. I wanted us to have a family and build a home and grow old together. If I lied to Bruno and said I'd stop seeing her, I won't have achieved anything.

He got to his feet. "The only thug around here is you."

"Don't come into my home and insult me. You're under my roof, you show me some respect."

"Your father's roof, you mean. If he wasn't dead, you'd be screwing around town, just like you always were, not a single responsibility on your shoulders."

"His death changed me. So, I guess that's something I have to thank your family for."

Bruno shook his head. "My family had nothing to do with that bomb going off."

"You expect me to believe you?"

"What reason do I have for lying?"

I hesitated for a moment. What reason *did* he have for lying? It would be a hell of a thing for him to use against me—maybe even a way to get me to hate Ivy, too, if she was involved in the planning.

But if it wasn't the Gilligans, who else could have been behind it?

I didn't want to get caught up in that right now. This was about me and Ivy.

"Fine, say whatever you want, but that doesn't change anything about the way I feel about your sister. You can break into my penthouse and threaten me all you want, but it won't make any difference."

He took a step forward. The beer bottle was still clenched in his hand, holding it by the neck. "I don't think you've heard me correctly. I'm not giving you an option. You're not to see my sister again."

"How exactly are you planning to stop me? I'd die before I stopped seeing her."

I wasn't sure I wanted to know the answer to that question. He wouldn't try to kill me, would he? Not right here in my home? What would he do? Steal a few things and try to make it look like a break-in? Or did he already have a plan to get rid of my body so he could just make it appear as though I'd vanished?

Bruno set the beer bottle down on the sideboard. "I can make that work."

"What? No coaster?" I commented.

The jibe was a distraction. I had a gun in the top drawer of the sideboard, but I was at least ten paces away from it. If Bruno was also armed—which I now suspected he was—I'd be dead before I got there.

It also occurred to me that I probably would have been better off lying about not seeing Ivy again than I was dead.

"Think what Ivy's going to say when she learns what you've done," I warned him.

He pulled out a flick knife. It was a relief. I stood a chance against a knife. Perhaps he'd just give me a warning cut then leave. At least it wasn't a gun.

He cocked his head. "If I do this right, she'll never have to know. You'll just simply be gone from her life. All problems solved."

Fuck. Did that mean he *did* intend on killing me?

I took a sidestep towards where the gun was kept.

I lifted both hands in surrender. "Okay, fine. You win. I won't see Ivy anymore."

"You expect me to believe that after the whole 'I want to marry her' bullshit?"

"Well, you're not giving me much choice here."

"I already gave you a choice, and you made the wrong one. Time's up, arsehole."

He lunged at me, brandishing the knife. I darted to one side, bringing up my elbow with the intention of knocking it from his grip. But he was young and fit, too, and he easily evaded me and then spun back around to face me. Fucker. He came at me again, knife held above his shoulder, ready to stab. He definitely didn't intend on only giving me a flesh wound. I drew back this time, but the knife came down in a sweeping arc and cut through the front of my shirt. I felt nothing for a second, then the pain came. I glanced down to see the shirt slicing and my skin flapping open, from above my breast bone down to my solar plexus.

Fuck. Blood ran down my skin.

I couldn't allow myself to be distracted. I understood fully now that Bruno Gilligan, while he swore he wasn't responsible for killing my father, was fully determined to kill me now. There was no point in me yelling for help—my apartment had been deliberately soundproofed from the rest of the hotel—and I didn't have time to get my phone out of my pocket and call for help.

We did a strange kind of dance, circling one another. I was overly aware that I only had my bare hands, while he had a knife.

Our circling brought me next to the sideboard where he'd put down the drink he'd taken from my fridge.

I snatched up the beer bottle and brought the bottom down hard on the surface. The glass smashed, leaving me with the neck and jagged remains in hand. I worked purely on instinct. I was hurt and bleeding and fighting for my life.

Bruno lunged at me again.

This time, I got under his arm, but not without him catching me with the knife across my shoulder. My movement brought me directly behind him. Before he got the chance to spin to face me, I grabbed his head from behind, yanking his chin up, and drew the broken glass across his throat.

Chapter Eighteen

Ivy

I stepped through my front door, and my mouth dropped open.

What the fuck?

Had I been robbed? The interior was a disaster. Even from my position in the entrance hall, it was obvious someone had tossed the place. Every drawer stood open or had been pulled fully out of the dresser and left on the floor, and the contents were strewn everywhere.

My heart rate skyrocketed, my skin prickling with goosebumps. I was afraid, but now wasn't the time to give in to that fear.

I was a Gilligan, and I wasn't going to be run out of my own home. After the experience with those two pricks outside the club, I was determined to defend myself. I couldn't have someone run in and save me every time there was trouble.

My first instinct was to call the police, but that wasn't how our family did things. Who the hell would be stupid enough to rob a Gilligan property? Had whoever done this left already? I strained my ears for any sound, but none came to me. I'd used my key to unlock the front door and I hadn't seen any sign of damage. Could they have come through a window?

Moving cautiously, I stepped farther into the flat. I scanned around, trying to figure out what might have been taken. To my surprise, my expensive flat-screen television was still in place, and my MacBook Pro was where I'd left it on the kitchen counter. This didn't make sense. Why would someone break in here and leave the most pricy items?

Before entering any farther, I reached for the gun I kept attached by a clip to the bottom of the hall console. It only took a flick of my finger to release it, and the weapon fell into my hand. I took it out and checked the safety was off. I already knew it was loaded—unless someone had had the foresight to empty the magazine and replace it, lulling me into a false sense of security. I still felt better with the weight of the weapon in my hand.

Where was Mara? I hoped she'd been out at the time of the break-in and I wasn't about to come across her body. That would kill me.

I checked the windows, going from the kitchen to the living room, to the bathroom to the bedroom. None were unlocked or had been broken or tampered with. Yet more drawers had been emptied, but I still couldn't pinpoint anything that had been taken.

How had they got in?

Realisation dawned on me.

Whoever did this had a key and decided to use it.

My family.

What the fuck had they been looking for? Something they clearly thought I was hiding from them. There was only one thing that would put them in a position where they'd come here uninvited and go through my stuff.

Jayden.

Did they suspect I had a key for his place—that I'd been letting myself in and out whenever I wanted?

Oh no. No, no, no.

My stomach dropped.

I'd had his key—and the one used on the lift—stuck to the base of my bedside table drawer. The drawer had been yanked completely from the stand. I grabbed it and flipped it over.

The key was gone.

Tears filled my eyes. There was only one reason I could think of for them to need that key, and that was if they intended on paying Jay a surprise visit.

I put down the gun and grabbed my phone. My hands were shaking, and I struggled to bring up Jay's number.

I clamped the phone to my ear as it rang. *Please pick up, please pick up.* Tears swam in my eyes. Had my family gone to pay him a visit because of us? I knew with certainty that was exactly what had happened. Had they gone already? Was I too late? I knew my family. They had the ability to make people disappear if they were causing them problems.

Would they dare make Jayden vanish?

I swore I'd never forgive them.

The phone rang out to answerphone. I debated whether to leave a message, but then it beeped. "Jay, please be careful. I think my family have taken the key you gave me. They could be on their way to your place or might even be there now. I'm coming over."

I ended the call.

What was the quickest way across London? It wasn't rush hour, but traffic was always bad in the city. I didn't think I could handle getting the Tube, though. I hurried outside and spotted a delivery driver on a motorbike. I ran out onto the road in front of him.

"I'll pay you a hundred quid to take me across the city."

His eyes widened behind his visor. "Seriously?"

"Yes. I promise." I fished into my pocket and took out the cash. I'd been taking money out of my account every day, storing up a supply for when Jay and I left.

He shrugged. "Fine, but I don't have a helmet for you."

"I don't care. I just need to get there, fast as you can. It's an emergency."

I climbed onto the bike behind him, and then we were off, weaving through the traffic. I clung tight to a complete stranger, adrenaline pouring through my veins. I didn't care about my own safety—all I cared about was making sure I got to Jay before my brothers and father did.

In less than fifteen minutes, we pulled up outside the hotel, and I threw myself off the back of the bike and ran for the door. I spotted the concierge, Fredrick, and shouted his name. I didn't care if people were staring. I looked around for any sign of my family, but there was none.

"I need to go up to Jay's apartment. I think he might be in trouble."

Fredrick knew exactly what kind of man he was working for and didn't even question me. Together, we hurried to the bank of lifts.

My heart raced. I was filled with the horrific certainty I was too late. How would I ever forgive them if they'd hurt Jay? I blinked back tears, but now wasn't the time to cry. If I was too late, there would be plenty of time for that after.

My mouth ran dry as the lift rose through the building. I bounced from foot to foot, anxious of get out of there and put a stop to whatever my family had planned.

Finally, we drew to a halt, and the doors slid open, revealing Jayden's open-plan penthouse.

The first thing I saw was Jayden, sitting on the edge of his sofa, a broken beer bottle dangling from his fingers. The second thing was the blood coating his hand, arms, and chest. The third was the body lying on the floor near his feet.

"What—?"

My brain went into shock, unable to process what I saw. The blood...? Was Jay hurt?

I took a couple of shaky steps closer. "Jay?"

He didn't look up at me.

My gaze was drawn to the body on the floor. I had no doubt the person was dead. The pool of blood surrounding the body was too big for them to have survived. But as I took in the back of the man's head, the wavy, light-brown hair, and the suit jacket, a fresh flicker of alarm sparked inside me. I blinked hard, wanting to somehow wipe away what I was seeing, but when my gaze alighted on the back of the man's arm and the rose-gold Bremont watch on his wrist that Bruno never took off, the certainty of the man's identity finally sank in.

"Bruno?"

The air left my lungs in a rush, and though I barely remembered crossing the floor, I found myself on my knees beside my dead brother.

"Bruno?" I grabbed the back of his jacket and shook him, as though I somehow expected to be able to wake him up. My panic and grief built, a tsunami of emotions that released from me in a scream of utter pain and horror. "No, God, no. Please, not this!"

I folded myself over my brother's back, somehow trying to protect him, even though I was far too late. I sobbed uncontrollably, balling Bruno's jacket into my fists. I was scarcely aware of the other two men in the room—Fredrick and Jay.

What had happened? I'd come here to save Jay's life but instead found my brother dead. How was this possible?

Jayden's voice broke through to me. "Ivy, I'm so sorry. He left me with no choice."

Jay had killed Bruno.

I lifted my head and launched at him, wild in my grief and fury and heartache, slapping at his chest and shoulders.

"No, no, no! How could you? How could you?"

Tears streamed down my face. There was nothing he could ever do to make this right again. He'd destroyed everything.

I continued to hit him, and he didn't even raise his hands to protect himself from my blows. He just sat there with his head hanging, his eyes shut, and I was sure I saw a tear slip from his eye and drip off the end of his nose.

"I'm sorry, Ivy. He came here to kill me. He gave me no choice."

I couldn't believe that. There was always a choice, wasn't there?

"You killed my brother! You killed him! You *murdered* him."

"No, Ivy. No."

I battered him with my fists. "Tell me it wasn't you, then. Tell me!"

I was screaming at him now. I couldn't bring myself to turn around and see Bruno's body again.

I wanted to collapse into Jayden's chest and sob against him, to feel his arms around me, holding me tight and offering me comfort, but how could I do that when he was the one who'd caused such pain?

Chapter Nineteen
Jayden

I didn't try to defend myself against Ivy's beating fists.

I felt numb inside, distanced from myself, as though none of this was really happening. I was vaguely aware that Fredrick was also here, watching on with stunned horror.

"I didn't have any choice," I said again, as though repeating myself would make her believe me.

I glanced down to the broken bottle in my hand and the dead man at my feet, his throat opened in a ragged wound.

The bottle fell from my fingers and smashed on the floor. The neck would be covered in my fingerprints, but I couldn't bring myself to care. Maybe I should go down for this. If it would make Ivy look at me again, I'd spend the rest of my life behind bars.

"You've ruined us, Jay. You've destroyed everything."

She dropped to her knees beside her brother and let out another wail of anguish that went right to my core.

Still, I didn't move.

Ivy somehow pulled herself together again, enough to look up at me. "I know what kind of man you are, Jayden Wynter. I've known it from the start, but I was blinded to it. I was so fucking stupid. How could I ever think someone like you would ever change? You wanted to be king of the city, and this is the price you were willing to pay. Me. My family. The people

I love. Those are the things you're willing to cast aside so you can get what you want."

There wouldn't be any police involved. That wasn't how people like us worked. We dealt with things ourselves, in the shadows.

I reached for her, my fingers brushing her arm, and she jerked away as though I'd burned her.

"Don't fucking touch me. I never want to see you again!"

The thought of my future without her in it was like a vast, empty void of nothingness. What would be the point in my days if I never got to see her smile, or hear her tell me about something that had happened in her day, or feel her small warm body around mine, holding me tight? I always swore I'd destroy anyone who hurt her, and yet it turned out I was that person. I didn't think I'd ever known such pain. My heart literally felt like it was shattering into pieces. Even after my father had been killed, I'd never known such utter devastation. I wanted to rewind time and take it back again. I'd let him kill me instead, rather than see Ivy go through this anguish.

What would she have done if I'd been the one left lying there and Bruno had been the one standing over my body with the smashed bottle in his hand? Would she have been equally distraught? Would she be pushing her brother out of her life?

It didn't matter. That wasn't what had happened. I was alive, and he was dead, and there was nothing I could do to change that.

My heart ached. I wanted to crouch beside her and pull her into my arms and hold her until the pain went away, but that wasn't going to happen. I could never take back what I'd done.

I turned towards Fredrick. "Get her out of here."

I didn't know what the fallout of this was going to be. Would the rest of her family come after me once they'd learned what had happened? The fact that Bruno had been killed in my penthouse surely proved that he was the one who'd come after me and not the other way around. I'd been forced to do what I had to protect myself. But reason didn't always work when people were furious and grief-stricken.

There were people I could call who would make bodies disappear, but I owed it to Ivy to let her bury her brother.

"No," she cried as Fredrick tried to haul her to her feet. "I'm not leaving him."

"Ivy, please," I begged her. "You can't stay here. You'll get him back, I promise."

I wanted nothing more than to hold her and tell her everything was going to be all right, but how could I? I didn't know that, and she'd already made it clear I was the last person she wanted comfort from. Not that it was surprising.

I'd rip my own heart out and hand it to her if I thought that would make things better.

Ivy was a sobbing mess, weakened by her grief. I hadn't expected her to leave, but Fredrick was able to guide her out of the penthouse.

Fuck. I felt empty inside. Hollowed out. But I couldn't just ignore the fact I had a dead body in my apartment. I needed to deal with it. I was also hurt and still bleeding, but I didn't think it was life-threatening.

Tam had his hands full with the baby and Hallie, so I called his brother, Leo.

I explained what had happened.

"Fuck," he said. "Fucking Gilligans."

I thought the same, if it wasn't for Ivy.

"What was he doing in your penthouse?"

"Does that matter?"

"It does if there are going to be repercussions for the rest of us."

I considered lying and saying I didn't know, and that this must have been part of their plan to destroy us, like the shooting of Harvey at the wedding or the bomb they'd planted, but what would have been the point? I didn't care if they tore me to shreds for it. Nothing they could do or say would make me feel any worse than I already did. Bruno had achieved what he'd wanted in the end, even if he wouldn't be around to appreciate it.

Ivy never wanted to see me again.

"I've been sleeping with his sister."

"What? What the fuck, Jay?"

"You can't say anything. What about you and Kaja? She's our enemy's daughter. This is no different."

From his silence, I could tell he knew I was right.

"What do you want me to do?"

"Help me clean up and then get the body to the Gilligans. I want Ivy to be able to bury her brother."

His disapproval came down the line. "That's not a good idea, Jay."

"I don't care. I'm doing it for Ivy. It's the least she deserves."

"You care about this girl then," he said. "It's not just fucking?"

"No. I love her, but now it's too late. Everything is fucked." I dragged my hand through my hair, clawing my nails into my scalp, deliberately hurting myself. "Maybe I should have just let Bruno kill me."

"I'll be there in twenty minutes. Let me contact a clean-up crew. It'll be like this never happened."

I highly doubted that, but I appreciated the support. A part of me just wanted to hand myself over to the Gilligans and tell them to finish the job. The only thing stopping me from doing so was Hallie and her baby. She deserved more. I couldn't put her through the same grief that Ivy was going through now.

Chapter Twenty

Ivy

Fredrick drove me to my father's house.

I sat on the back seat of the Range Rover, in the same place I'd given my virginity to Jay, staring down at the dried blood on my hands and clothes. My brother's blood. I alternated between being overwhelmed with unimaginable pain and being numb with grief. I wasn't going back to my place. I needed to be with what remained of my family, to tell them what had happened and to try to figure out what would happen next.

They had been in my house, had tossed the place for the key to Jay's place. I didn't know if Bruno had acted alone or if my other brother and father had something to do with it, too. I was furious with them for putting this chain of events into motion, but I was too heartsick to hate them for it. I'd lost Jayden now, as well as my brother, and I couldn't comprehend how I was going to get through each day. But I knew if I didn't do something, and fast, my family would want their revenge. As much as I hated Jayden for what he'd done, I couldn't let them kill him as well.

The concierge stopped outside the modern concrete-and-glass, multi-million-pound house I indicated to him.

"I hope you'll be okay," he said as I climbed out of the vehicle.

I just nodded, unable to speak. I slammed the door shut behind me. I could barely think straight. My entire head felt stuffy from all the crying, my eyes stung, and I struggled to breathe. My legs barely carried me to the front gate where I rang the buzzer over and over. He'd be able to see me on the security monitor and know to let me in.

Sure enough, the smaller part of the gate clicked open, and I pushed my way through.

My father, Greyson Gilligan, appeared on the doorstep. He must have seen the blood as his eyes widened.

"Ivy? What the fuck has happened?"

I didn't want to tell him this news while we were standing outside, but I couldn't stop it bursting from my mouth. "Bruno's dead."

His face paled. "What?"

I covered my face with my hands, not caring about the dried blood on my skin, and started to cry again.

He put his hand on my shoulder, ushering me indoors, and shut the door behind us. He guided me into the kitchen and forced me to take a seat. I hitched a breath and sniffed and pulled myself together enough to speak.

"He went to warn Jayden Wynter off me, and things went wrong. Jay killed him."

That he didn't question the reason why Bruno had gone to warn off Jayden told me he already knew Bruno had gone there, and so was aware of the relationship.

His hands balled into fists. A muscle tightened in his jaw. But the lack of emotion he showed at the news was unnerving.

"Then the Wynter boy will have to pay."

I knew exactly what that meant. "Please, you can't kill him."

My father glared at me. "You're begging for the life of a man who murdered your brother in cold blood."

"I'm begging for the life of another human being. I don't want to lose anyone else. I can't bear the thought. How many people have to die before we say enough is enough? Are we just going to kill and kill and kill until no one is left? What do you think is going to happen if you take your revenge on Jayden Wynter? You know about the alliance between the Wynters and the Cornells. Tam Cornell isn't going to sit back and let you kill Jayden. Tam is married to Jay's sister. They'll want payback."

"So you want us to do nothing?"

"No, I want you to grieve, like a normal person. I want you to help us heal. Or else where will it end? Will you be happy when one of them kills me next?"

"Of course not."

I babbled on, tears streaming down my cheeks. "Because that's what's going to happen. Maybe not tomorrow or even a month from now, but someday soon I'll be the one lying on the mortuary slab, and will you be happy about your revenge then?"

"Don't say that, Ivy."

I threw up both hands. "Why not? It's the truth, isn't it? Money and power is more important to you than family. It always has been, it always will be. Even losing your son isn't enough to change that."

"You don't understand."

"You're right, I don't. I'll never put money before the people I love, and now I've lost two of them."

"You loved that Wynter boy?" He curled his lip in disgust.

I didn't know how I was supposed to feel. I had loved him—with every inch of my being—but how could I hold onto that love now? I couldn't just turn that love off like a switch. It didn't work that way. I'd never felt so conflicted in my life. I was being torn in two—my head telling me to hate him for what he'd done, while my heart desperately wanted to go to him for comfort.

"I'm ashamed of you, Ivy. You need to know where your loyalties lie."

I shook my head. "Well, I'm ashamed of you, too. If you'd just accepted that Jayden and I were together, none of this would have happened. I know Bruno only went there to warn him off. Knowing Bruno, he wouldn't have just accepted it when Jay refused to stop seeing me either."

His jaw hardened, and his gaze slipped down to the floor. "We don't know the reason Bruno was there."

He was lying, I knew it. But what could I do? My family were suffering, and Jayden was the cause. I'd lost my brother at his hand, and that was something that could never be undone or made right again, though my chest ached and my eyes burned with tears at the thought.

"The only reason Bruno was anywhere near Jayden was because of me. Don't you think people are going to realise that? I'll be the one at fault."

"That's bullshit, Ivy, and you know it."

"Do I? Will they? Are you happy to take that risk? Because if you're content to gamble with my life, then go ahead, kill Jayden Wynter, but don't think for a second that the Cornells won't see me as fair payment. They have that alliance for a reason. Jayden's sister, Hallie, is married to Tam Cornell—they have a family together now—and she won't just sit back and let you kill her brother. She'll get the Cornells to avenge him."

I barely knew how I was functioning. All I wanted was to go to my bed, crawl beneath the covers, and cry myself into unconsciousness, but I couldn't let myself break until I knew Jay was safe. My emotions warred inside me. Jay had killed my brother, and maybe my father was right and I should want him dead, but how could I want someone else I loved to die?

Because I did love him—that was the truth of it. I could never excuse what he'd done, and I could never even bring myself to look at him again, never mind forgive him, but I couldn't just switch my emotions on and off.

My father caught me by both hands, surprising me. "I love you, Ivy. You're my only daughter. I've just lost one child and I don't want to lose another. I still want Jayden Wynter dead, but if it means I won't lose you as well, then I'll let him live."

I exhaled a hitched sob and allowed him to pull me against his chest while I cried.

Chapter Twenty-One
Jayden

I was dead inside, and every day was torture.

A month had passed since I'd killed Bruno Gilligan. A month since I'd last seen Ivy. A month since she'd said she never wanted to see me again.

What was I supposed to do without her? Everything else had fallen into the background. My drive to rule the city had died a death, but my rage hadn't subsided. The difference was that now I didn't care who I took down with me. I'd lost Ivy, and that was all I cared about.

The only distraction I had was Hallie and the new baby. I loved having a baby niece, but I was fearful that the poison running through my veins would somehow harm her, too. Because everything I touched turned to hell.

I'd shed no tears for Bruno Gilligan. That arsehole had it coming, and it had been a case of me or him. But the loss of Ivy had torn my heart from my chest. Seeing that horror and grief in her eyes, watching her piece together what had happened and realising I was the one responsible for her brother's death, was enough to leave me torturing myself, day after day. It didn't matter that I'd been defending myself. I wasn't sure she'd even heard me say it. All that mattered was that her brother was dead and I'd been the one to cause it.

I scanned the bar I'd just walked into for the biggest of the men here—not just the biggest, but the meanest-looking, too. I knew I wasn't exactly a small man myself, and, with my tattoos, people came to view me as being tough. Maybe they were right, but I wanted someone to think they could take me on. Making sure I'd had a skinful was a good way of doing that. If someone thought I was too drunk to throw a punch, they were more likely to jump into the fight.

A bloke who was well over six feet and probably spent far too much time in the gym stood at the bar, his attention focused on a fake-tanned, skinny blonde beside him.

I pushed in so I was next to the blonde, deliberately nudging her with my shoulder. Her blue eyes widened slightly upon seeing me. I still drew a woman's eye, even if I had no interest in them anymore.

"All right, darling," I said, jerking my chin at her. "Buy you a drink?"

Her jaw dropped. "Umm, no thanks."

She raised her eyebrows at her boyfriend as though she couldn't believe my nerve.

"Come back to mine then, and I'll open a bottle of champagne. You can't be seriously into that guy. He looks like he's on 'roids, and we all know what that does to a man's cock."

I lifted my hand and wiggled my little finger to demonstrate the point.

He took the bait. "What the fuck did you just say?"

"Just thought the lady here might want to know what it's like to ride a man with a decent-sized cock."

I grabbed the front of my jeans and put on a fake leer. I had no interest in his girlfriend, but I didn't need him to know that.

"Fuck you, dickhead."

Muscles pushed forward, moving his girlfriend to one side to plant himself in between me and her. I took a step back from the bar, not wanting to get anyone else involved.

"Who the fuck are you calling a dickhead?" I said, then snorted. "But at least I have one. You really need to lay off those steroids or your girl is going to find her way into my bed, and, when she discovers how it feels to get properly fucked and not be able to walk for a week, she's definitely not going to come back to you."

His face gradually turned beetroot, his nostrils flaring, a tic flexing in his jaw. His shoulders straightened, and his biceps bulged. He was like a racehorse caught in the starting block just waiting for that whistle to go. All it needed was that final push.

"I'm going to smash your fucking face in," he threatened.

I laughed. "I'd like to see you try."

I knew it was coming but I didn't bother to duck out of the way, however easy that would have been for me. His meaty fist collided with my jawbone, sending my head rocking backwards. Pain flashed through my face, and my teeth clanked together, narrowly missing my tongue. I had to blink several times to get my vision to straighten.

I wanted this. I deserved this. It was what I was here for.

Despite the power behind the punch, I didn't go down.

I wiped my hand across my cheek, enjoying the pain. "Is that all you've got? You're showing yourself up in front of your girl."

He snarled and swung for me again. This punch caught the side of my nose, and a satisfying crunch sounded in my ears. The pain intensified, and I relished in it, wallowed in it. It was exactly what I'd come here for.

"More!" I roared, slamming my fists against my chest. "Come on, mate. Fucking show me what you've got."

Muscles lifted his fist and then hesitated. Did he see the madness in my eyes?

Blood poured from my nose, dripping down the front of my shirt and onto the floor. I smiled at the sight. With any luck, I'd keep bleeding until I passed out, and then I wouldn't have to think any more.

It dawned on me that Muscles didn't want to hit me again.

"What are you waiting for?" I spat a large glob of blood and snot at his feet. "Fucking hit me."

Muscles twitched, but he lowered his arm.

My heart sank, but I kept up the bravado. "Come on, what's it going to take? You want me to bend your girlfriend over the bar and show her what it's like to have a big cock in her cunt?"

I was ashamed of myself for using the girl like this, but I couldn't seem to stop. I *couldn't* stop. I was still very much conscious. The pain wasn't enough. I deserved more—so much more.

The blonde touched Muscle's arm and shook her head. "Let's get out of here."

He turned back to her and looped his arm around her shoulders.

"You're fucked up, mate. Get some therapy."

The two left together, and I just stood there, dripping blood on the floor, my face throbbing with the beat of my heart. The pub had fallen into silence, and I sensed the eyes of the patrons who remained all trained on me, probably wondering what I was going to do next.

What *was* I going to do next?

The police had probably been called by now, but I didn't care too much about that either. So what if I ended up behind bars? It made no difference to me now. My whole life felt like a jail cell now I no longer had Ivy in it.

The barman cleared his throat. "You should probably leave."

He was right.

The adrenaline had seeped from me, and now the pain in my face was my main focus. That was fine by me. Physical pain, I could deal with. It was all the emotional torment I was in right now that I couldn't handle. I considered picking a fight with someone else—get them to finish the job—but I couldn't muster the energy. Maybe I should just step outside the pub doors, onto the street, and then walk out in front of a bus or something. What a way to go. But knowing my luck, that wouldn't take me out either, and I'd end up paralysed or some shit like that, trapped inside my own head to torture myself forevermore.

That wasn't a risk worth taking.

The stupid thing was that I still nursed a tiny spark of hope inside me that somehow things would change and Ivy would come back to me. Some days, I thought that spark had completely died and all that was left was a black nothingness, but other days it flickered back to life.

When that hope went out completely, then it would be time to call it a day.

Chapter Twenty-Two

Ivy

I was heartbroken. Not just broken, shattered into a million pieces. I couldn't even bring myself to get out of bed, never mind take a shower or brush my teeth. I knew my other family members moved around the house sometimes, but they might as well have been ghosts.

I didn't care about my degree. I knew I could do my exams next year instead, but I didn't want to. What was the fucking point? Everything was ruined now.

I missed Jayden and hated him in equal measures. The emotions warred inside me. How could I ever forgive him? I couldn't. It was as simple as that. If I did, I would lose the rest of my family, too. My father and surviving brother would never forgive me, and I couldn't blame them. It had only been my begging for Jayden's life that had prevented them killing him already.

Someone had come into my bedroom and was now moving around, picking things up and opening the curtains.

"Come on, Ivy," Mara said. "It's been a month now. You have to get up."

A month. It couldn't have been a month already, surely? A couple of weeks I could accept, but not a month.

I suddenly thought of something.

When had I last had my period?

Oh, fuck.

How could we be so fucking irresponsible?

Did I feel any differently? I pressed my fingers to my breasts, probing carefully. They felt a little swollen and tender but no more so than they normally did before I got my period. There was a low ache in my belly, too, but again, that was normal. I wasn't nauseous or anything like that. Maybe my period was just late. It would be understandable, considering all the stress I'd been under and dealing with my grief.

My heart rate galloped. I wouldn't be able to rest until I knew for sure.

But the thought of getting up and dressing and leaving the house felt like a monumental task. I didn't care what I looked like, but I had enough self-worth that I didn't want to go out smelling of body odour and with bad breath.

I was probably just late. The lure of that lie was compelling. If I told myself it was nothing to worry about, I could close my eyes and go to sleep again. I wouldn't need to take a shower or get dressed. I wouldn't need to think about how much I missed Jayden, or Bruno, or how there was nothing I could ever do to change things or roll back time.

I curled back up under my covers, aware the sheets were stale and needed washing, just like everything else.

"Ivy!" Mara's stern voice broke through to me. "I'm not going until you've got out of bed. Bruno is dead, but you're still alive. I won't let you throw everything away."

I was still alive, but it was a life that would never have Jay in it. I'd tasted what it was like to have that kind of intense passion, and now the thought of trying to continue with that missing was too much.

My world had drained of colour.

She yanked back my duvet, and I groaned and reached for it again.

"No." She held it tight. "You are not staying in bed. Something needs to change. This is not how you're going to live your life."

"I'm tired," I groaned.

"You're depressed," she counteracted, "and that's completely understandable, considering what's happened, but there are things you can do to help that. See a doctor, get some meds, if you need to, but start with a shower and sort your hair out, and brush your teeth."

A doctor. Meds. I wouldn't be able to take anything if I was pregnant, would I? I had no idea how these things worked.

I squeezed my eyes shut. *I'm not pregnant, my period is just late.*

Images of the number of times I'd had sex with Jayden unprotected flashed through my head. Every caress, every kiss, every time afterwards when we'd held each other, our foreheads pressed together, wrapped in each other's arms. Those were the painful memories, the ones that made my chest ache and made me feel like I would never run out of tears. But every time I missed him, I was tormented with guilt.

How could I miss the man who'd murdered my brother? What kind of person did that make me?

She wasn't giving up. "Come on, Ivy. I'm serious. I'm not going to leave until you do."

I shut my eyes again and didn't move.

She let out a sigh, and for a moment, I thought she'd gone, but then I heard the thunder of the shower running.

Her hand clamped around my arm. "I told you I wasn't giving up."

"What are you doing?"

"Getting you out of bed."

I hadn't been eating much since everything had happened. The meals she brought me pretty much went uneaten, apart from the most basic of foods, such as soup and toast, just enough to keep me alive. But my lack of eating meant I'd also lost a fair amount of weight—I guessed that could also account for my late period—and it made it easier for her to move me. She was a wide, stocky woman, and easily hauled me out of bed.

"Mara, no!"

"I told you I wasn't taking no for an answer."

She hauled me across the bedroom, towards the bathroom. The sound of the shower grew louder as we got closer.

I was still in my silk pyjamas, but she didn't seem to care. She slid open the glass door of the shower and shoved me inside. I gasped as the water hit the top of my head and shoulders, soaking through the thin material of my pyjamas. I guessed I should at least be grateful the water wasn't cold.

"Mara, you cow!"

"You can call me names all you want. I'd rather that than no reaction from you."

"Fine. I'm in now. I'll wash. You can leave."

She put her hands on her robust hips and shook her head. "Nice try, but I'm not going anywhere. I'm standing here until you've washed yourself and your hair, and then I'll let you get out."

"I need to strip off if I'm going to wash properly."

She turned her back on me. "Get on with it then. It's nothing I haven't seen before."

I was tempted to just sink to my backside in the shower tray and sit there until she went away—she couldn't stand there forever—but deep down, I knew she was right. I'd been paralysed by my grief for so long, and while I knew there was no time limit on grieving, that niggling worry in the back of my mind about my late period gave me a reason to do as she said.

With a sigh, I turned to face the shower spray, and peeled off my now wet PJs. I dropped them into the stall to deal with later. I'd tackle my hair first. The scent of the shampoo lifted my mood a fraction, and scrubbing the suds into my scalp felt good, too. My head had been itchy for some time now, and I was relieved that it wouldn't feel that way anymore. I rinsed the shampoo and then used some conditioner. Without rinsing it out, I used my Denman brush on the numerous knots. Parts of my hair were like dreadlocks, and I wasn't sure I'd have the energy to work them out, but I kept going, knowing that if I didn't, I'd have to cut big chunks off my hair.

I rinsed the conditioner out and then turned my attention to my body. Using a good dollop of a citrus-scented gel, I washed my skin.

My hand brushed over my tender breasts and down to my belly. Could I really have a new life growing in there? A life that was half Jayden Wynter. I closed my eyes, bracing myself against the fresh wave of pain washing over me. I didn't know how to process the possibility. It was better not to think about it.

As I switched off the shower, Mara grabbed a towel from the heated rail and handed it over to me. I wrapped it around my body, and then she gave me a second, smaller one for my hair, which I knotted on top of my head.

"See," she said, eyeing me up. "Better already."

"I think it's going to take a lot more than a shower, Mara."

"I know, sweetheart, and I'm sorry. I'm only doing it because I care about you."

Tears threatened again. They always seemed to be close these days.

"I know."

She was the only one who cared about me. Other than at Bruno's funeral—which had been a private affair, with only family present, and the crematorium paid off—I'd barely seen my father or Aiden. Neither of them had bothered to visit to see how I was.

My remaining family hated me now. I knew they blamed me, at least in part, for Bruno's death. I'd brought Jayden into our lives, and if I hadn't been seeing him, Bruno would still be alive. They were right, too. I blamed myself.

Still, I found myself going back over those moments after I'd found Bruno's body.

Jay had tried to talk to me afterwards. He'd said that Bruno had been the one to attack him and he'd only been defending himself, but that didn't change the outcome. Bruno probably did go and confront Jay about us, but would he have killed him? I didn't know. I didn't want to believe my brother would try to murder the man I loved, but it wasn't as though they weren't capable of killing.

Wasn't that why I'd been so afraid of them finding out in the first place?

I dressed in the loosest, most comfortable clothes I had—an oversized t-shirt and hoody and a pair of sweatpants, and added a pair of fluffy socks. I blow-dried the worst of the wetness out of my hair and then tied it back to keep it out of my face. I didn't bother with makeup—I didn't care how I looked, and I hoped no one would see me anyway. At least I was clean.

The effort of showering and getting dressed had sucked all the energy from me, and I found myself sitting on the edge of my bed again, my hands in my lap, my head hanging. I knew I was depressed, but it wasn't something that pills could fix. Therapy would probably have been a better bet, but how could I possibly go and talk to someone about what had happened? For one, I'd be admitting that Jay had murdered Bruno and I couldn't say that out loud to anyone. As much as I wanted to trust the people we had on our payroll, there was nothing stopping someone from using that information against me. Or against Jayden.

"I hate this life, Mara," I said. "I hate this city. I want to leave, but I'm frightened of being on my own, and I don't know where I should go. I've never lived anywhere else."

She sat beside me. "There's a whole world out there. You're young and free. You could go anywhere."

"I'm afraid of being lonely."

"It's okay to be lonely sometimes. That's often when we learn who we truly are as people."

I sniffed. "Maybe that's what I'm most worried about—finding out who I am. What if I don't like that person?"

"Why would you not?"

"Because I got my brother killed, and the man I loved was forced to kill him."

"Oh, sweetheart." She covered my hand with hers. "You're not responsible for the things men do."

"I miss him. I miss them both, and I feel terrible for that."

"You loved him?"

"I still do, and what kind of person does that make me?"

"An honest one. You can't turn off love because of one act, no matter how terrible that act might have been."

"I wish I could."

"You're young," she said again, as though trying to drill it home. "You won't feel this way forever, even if it doesn't feel that way right now. Time, while it doesn't make grief go away, it does lessen the impact. It won't always feel so raw."

I looked over at her. "And love? Does time make that lessen the impact, too?"

"You probably don't want to hear this, but you will meet someone else and love again one day."

"You're right, I don't want to hear it. I'll never put myself through this kind of pain again. Never."

"Sweetheart, not everyone lives this kind of life."

"But I do, though. It's what I was born into, and even if I tried to leave, it would follow me somehow."

My eyes filled with tears again. I didn't know how it was possible to cry so much without drying out. I'd cried myself to sleep every night, and then, when I'd woken and remembered what had happened, I'd cried again. My chest was a hollow ball where my heart had once been, and I couldn't ever see myself feeling whole again. I longed to be able to go back in time and change what had happened, and some part of me felt it was so unfair that I couldn't do it—the frustration of not being able to change things mentally wearing me down.

Stupidly, a part of me even hoped Jayden would get in touch. Though I knew it would be no good for me and would only open old wounds, I still found myself checking my phone hoping to see his name on the screen. I had almost messaged him countless times, typing out huge messages, pouring my heart and soul into those words. But I had always managed to delete the message before sending it—the sensible part of me aware that I couldn't open up this line of communication again. Nothing he ever did or said would make things any better.

I needed to muster a little extra energy. There was something I needed to do or else I wasn't sure I'd sleep again. I had to know one way or another.

"I'm going for a walk," I told Mara. "Just round the block. I won't go far."

Her brow creased in concern. "Do you want me to come?"

"No, but thank you. I need a little time to myself."

"You've been by yourself too much," she said, somewhat disapprovingly.

"Baby steps," I told her, forcing myself to my feet.

I left my house and stepped out onto the street, inhaling fresh air into my lungs for the first time in a month. It seemed too busy out here, too loud, too everything. I wanted to vanish. Instead, I put my hands in my pockets and ducked my head, allowing my hair to fall over my face. I didn't want anyone to recognise me, especially considering where I was going and what I was about to do. I walked to the high street and slipped into the local chemist. With my head still down, I found the aisle that contained the pregnancy tests.

My hand shook as I selected one of the popular brands, one that would leave no doubt as to what the result was, and I took it up to the counter.

"Anything else?" the woman serving asked me.

I shook my head. "No, just this one."

I hoped she wasn't going to start asking me any questions. Mercifully, she didn't, and I left the shop again, stuffing the test into the sleeve of my hoody so it wouldn't be seen.

Back at the house, I went to the bathroom and sat on the toilet. I unwrapped the pregnancy test and quickly checked the instructions, though there wasn't exactly much to it.

I peed on the stick. My heart felt like it was in my throat, and I was lightheaded and breathless.

The worst part was that I didn't know what I wanted the result to be.

It was pathetic, to still want that connection to him. It would give me a reason to have to contact him again, even though I knew how painful that would be. But even having that thought filled me with overwhelming guilt again. I couldn't wish a baby into this world just so I could be in touch with a man who'd killed my brother. What kind of sick person was I? I didn't want to think about what that would do to my family, as well. They were going through their own grief and didn't need this complication. What if they said I'd have to get rid of it? Or have the baby but then give it up for adoption? They'd never allow Jayden to have the child.

Without looking at the test, I balanced it on the edge of the sink and then set my timer on my phone to the allocated amount. I promised myself I wouldn't check it until the time was up. I didn't want to give myself false hope, either way.

I sat with my head in my hands, trying not to wallow, and failing.

The alarm sounded on my phone, and I sat up straight, swallowing my fear. With my hand shaking, I reached for the stick.

I stared at the result and burst into tears.

Chapter Twenty-Two
Jayden

I woke from a troubled sleep with thudding in my temples and a throbbing face. I managed to ease open one gritty eye and swiftly shut it again as daylight hit the back of my eyeball.

My mouth tasted sour from the amount of alcohol I'd consumed, and the only way I'd feel vaguely tolerable was if I started drinking again. Unfortunately, I had a distinct memory of draining my last whiskey bottle dry during the early hours, so if I wanted more booze, I was going to need to leave the penthouse.

Then I remembered I lived in a hotel. I could call up fucking room service if I wanted.

I hated that I was conscious again. All I wanted was to vanish back into sleep.

There were times I dreamed of her, where we were back together again, and the terrible thing that had happened had been the dream—no, the nightmare. We made love, and I'd praise her while I was fucking her until she'd climaxed, and then I'd come, too, and the intensity of it would wake me. Then I'd discover myself alone and broken-hearted, and with sheets wet with cum.

I struggled to see what the point was of me being in the world. The only reason I could think of was being here for Hallie and my niece, but even then I wondered if they were better off without me. What if I did something that hurt them in the same way I'd managed to hurt Ivy?

During the days and weeks after it had happened, I'd expected Greyson and Aiden Gilligan to come for me. I'd been ready for them, too—but I wouldn't have fought back. I'd have stood there with my arms open wide and let them do what they wanted. Then they hadn't come, and I could only assume Ivy had something to do with that. Had she begged for my life? If so, did that mean she still felt something for me?

The Cornells were losing their patience with me, and I couldn't say I blamed them. I hadn't shown up for any of the business meetings I'd put in place the previous month and didn't bother to return any calls. They'd cut me some slack at first, but I didn't know how long that would last.

I didn't even care.

The nasty taste in my mouth made me want to gag, so I forced my eyes open again and managed to drag my sorry arse into the bathroom. I turned on the shower and stood beneath the water, letting it run over the top of my head. I closed my eyes against the flow, water rolling over my eyelids, dripping off my lashes. I thought of the number of times I'd fucked Ivy in this shower, how beautiful she'd always looked with her skin wet and flushed, her hair dripping down her back.

Blood rushed to my cock, and I forced the thought away. Making myself come with a head full of images of her was like the worst possible torture. All it did was remind me of what I'd never have, and it tore my heart from my chest all over again.

I washed myself down and then got out of the shower and scrubbed my teeth. I felt a little closer to human now, so at least

I could go out in public. I didn't want to use room service to bring me up a bottle of something, aware the staff would talk.

I threw on some clothes and raked my fingers through my wet hair. I appeared decent enough for someone to serve me alcohol, and not some homeless person on the street who clearly had a drinking problem.

The buzzer sounded for the lift.

I didn't even care who was here—definitely not enough to bother checking who it was. If it was someone here to put an end to me, I'd most likely greet them with open arms. I allowed the lift to rise and waited for the doors to open. In a way, it would be a blessing if there was an armed man on the other side of those doors.

But, as they slid open, it wasn't a man standing there but a beautiful young woman with wavy blonde hair and bright-blue eyes. She had lost weight since I'd last seen her, her cheekbones sharp, her eyes even more soulful than before. She was so tiny and fragile, I almost wanted to shut the lift doors again, if only to protect her from me.

"Ivy?"

"Hello, Jay."

I had to stop myself comically rubbing my eyes, wondering if I was seeing things. "What are you doing here?"

"I need to talk to you. It's important."

Okay, so she wasn't here to kill me.

"Come in. Sit down." I guided her into the kitchen-dining area and dragged a chair out from the table. "It's so good to see you."

She didn't say it was good to see me, too, but that was hardly surprising.

Perhaps she was here to deliver my punishment herself. Maybe she'd brought a knife, just as her brother had done, and now she was going to slit my throat as payback.

If that was her plan, I would lift my chin for her but keep my eyes open, so the last thing I ever got to see was her beautiful face.

Chapter Twenty-Three
Ivy

None of the feelings I'd had for him had faded over the past couple of months. Seeing him again was like someone had punched me in the chest, bruising my already fragile heart and stealing my breath. He was so beautiful, perhaps even more so because of the pain I saw in his eyes. I wanted to go to him, the pull was almost impossible to fight. Everything felt wrong to have space between us, both physical and emotional.

I hadn't realised how much I'd missed him until I was with him again. I wanted to wrap my arms around his neck and bury my face against his skin and inhale that familiar scent of him.

I trembled from nerves. How did he feel about me now? What was going through his head? Was seeing me here having the same emotional impact on him as it was me, or was he cold inside, everything he might have once felt for me gone?

He'd brought me into the kitchen-dining area instead of the living room, where Bruno had died. Had he done that deliberately, or was it an unconscious action? I glanced down at his hands—hands that had once given me nothing but pleasure—and tried to marry them with the idea of the violence that had led to my brother's death. I'd expected to see a monster when I looked at him, but I didn't.

He was still just Jay.

My stomach churned with nerves at the news I'd brought with me.

I hadn't told anyone the truth of my predicament. How could I?

The thought of going up to either my brother or father and saying 'Hey, guess what, I'm pregnant, and the father is the man who murdered Bruno' left me sick with nerves.

The first thing they'd do is tell me to get rid of it, but I couldn't do that. This was a part of Jayden I carried inside me, and I'd no more get rid of it than I would cut off my own leg.

But I was fearful of what extremes this news might push them to.

Would they hurt me to cause a miscarriage? They'd never laid a finger on me before, but I knew this news would push them to the edge. Or maybe they'd poison me to try to rid me of the baby.

Or I could just not tell them.

Eventually, they were going to notice the changes in my body, but that wouldn't happen for months. It wasn't as though they were focused on me anyway. They were both still grief-stricken. My father had thrown himself into work, and my brother was out drinking every night. The drinking frightened me more than the work. What if he came across Jay one night while he was out and they'd both been on the booze? They'd promised not to kill Jay because I'd begged them not to, but also because he was in cahoots with the Cornells now, and killing Jayden Wynter would mean the end of our family, too. But if my brother had had a skinful and came across Jay, he might not be thinking straight. In fact, I knew he wouldn't be.

I could only hope that by the time my pregnancy got too obvious to hide, months would have passed and Bruno's loss might not be so raw.

Though I tried to relax in the seat, my entire body was wound into a knot of tension. I clasped my hands together, my shoulders tense. I had no idea how Jayden was going to react to my news.

He took a seat in the chair beside me and then twisted it to face me. "How have you been?"

"Terrible," I said. "You?"

"Terrible," he echoed.

I almost wanted to smile. I was glad he'd been having a hard time of things. He looked awful—not only because of the swelling and bruises across his face—but because of a sadness that seemed to exude from his pores. It didn't make me love him any the less, however. How could it? He'd killed my brother, but I still fucking loved him.

"What happened to your face?"

He touched the bridge of his nose and winced. "Oh, bar fight."

"You're still going to bars then?" His words stung. Was he going out to try to pick up women? I hadn't even thought about being with another man. I wasn't sure it was something I'd *ever* think about.

"Only so I can get into fights."

My voice came out as a croak. "I wanted you to fight for me. You walked away too easily."

He lifted his bruised eyes to mine. "I was trying to fight for you, Ivy. That's what I was doing when...it happened."

I tried to blink away my tears. "You were fighting for me?"

His face was crumpled in pain. "He told me I wasn't ever allowed to contact you again. I told him I'd die first, so he said then that's what would have to happen."

"He said he would kill you if you didn't stay away from me?" I wanted to make sure I understood right.

He nodded. "And I had no intention of ever saying that I would stay away from you. I could no more have done that than cut off my own head."

"You have stayed away from me," I pointed out. "For a month now."

"Only because I knew you wouldn't have wanted me anywhere near you. I wasn't going to let your family tell me to stay away from you, but you saying it is a whole different thing."

I *had* told him to stay away from me. I told him I never wanted to see him again. I'd meant it at the time, too, of course I had. At least a part of me had. How could I possibly reconcile my feelings of grief and hatred with love? But now it wasn't just about me and my feelings. There were more important things to consider.

As so often happened recently, without me even thinking about it, my hand slipped to my stomach, protectively cupping the barely visible bump hidden beneath my shirt.

Jayden's gaze slipped down to my belly, and his eyes widened.

"Ivy?"

I realised he'd seen. There was no point in trying to hide anything. It was the reason I was here talking to him.

My voice was a breathless whisper, and the tears were back. "Yes. I'm pregnant."

"Oh my God. Ivy."

He leaned without even waiting for me to say it was what I wanted and scooped me into a hug, pulling me onto his lap. The embrace I'd imagined when I'd first seen him came to life, and I clutched the back of his shirt and buried my nose in his neck. He did the same, and we clung to one another like two people drowning. God, he felt so good. His warmth, his scent, the pressure of his arms around my body, his hot breath against my skin. Everything about him was right—like I'd finally come home—and it made me want to cry.

My heart ached, but how could I forgive him? Could I ever forgive him?

"A baby," he said. "We're having a baby."

I forced myself to lean away from him so I could look into his eyes. "Are we? How can we possibly make this work, Jay? I'm not sure I'll ever get over what happened."

He set his jaw. "That baby is ours. I won't listen to a second of you trying to convince yourself that you shouldn't have it. We both know that isn't what you want. I know you, Ivy. You want a family. You want *us* to be a family."

Tears filled my eyes, and I swallowed hard against the painful lump in my throat. "How can we be? You don't understand how hard this is for me."

"No, maybe I don't, not fully, and I don't expect you to ever forgive me for what I did. But that doesn't make me incapable of taking care of you." He placed his palm over mine and my stomach. "And taking care of whatever little person you're growing inside you."

I closed my eyes briefly, allowing myself to picture a world where this was normal and natural. I wanted it so badly, but could I ever bring myself to forgive him, or if not forgive him, somehow allow myself to leave what had happened in the past?

Emotions battled silently inside me.

I emptied my lungs of air. "The Cornells are pushing my family out of the city, and that's fine by me. I don't care. My father and brother blame me for getting involved with you. They think if I hadn't then Bruno would still be alive, and maybe they're right."

He shook his head. "It's not your fault."

"I'm not so sure about that. I chose to get involved with you, even though, deep down, I always knew it would result in something like this happening."

"You couldn't predict the future."

"But I did." I sighed again. "I want a normal life, Jay. I want this baby to have a normal life. I don't want him or her to grow up wondering if someone they fall in love with is going to end up shot one day, or if they're going to lose one of us or a sibling to violence."

"What are you saying?"

"Before this happened, we'd already planned on leaving. Maybe we should stick to that plan?"

His eyes widened a fraction. "You want to leave?"

"I want to get far away from here, away from London. I don't even care where—maybe Cornwall or even Scotland. Somewhere with fields and wildlife, and in a village where everyone knows everyone else and says good morning to each other. I want our son or daughter to go to a tiny school and get invited to their friends' houses for tea."

He squeezed my hands.

"Baby, I would follow you to the ends of the earth if it meant we were together again. I'm nothing without you. My life is nothing."

I blinked back tears. "Really?"

"Of course. And what about us? What would we do?"

"Whatever we wanted. Neither of us need any more money than we already have. If we get bored, we could look at starting up a little business—a legitimate business."

"Or we could have another baby?" he suggested.

I couldn't help the smile tweaking my cheeks. "Or that."

He grew serious, his teeth digging into his lower lip. "Are you ever going to get to a point where you can look at me and not see the person who killed your brother?"

I pressed my lips together and glanced down, trying to figure out how to put my mixed thoughts and emotions into words.

"Honestly," I started, "I'm not sure, but I'm willing to work on it. What happened wasn't completely your fault. You didn't go out that day planning to kill Bruno. I know that. What we have together is too important to throw away. We're going to be a family."

"What about your father and brother?"

"They're losing their grip on North London, and they know it. Tam Cornell and the business you've put in place is too powerful for them. They're going to be left scrabbling over a few pickings, and that's not what they want either. The time is up for the Gilligans in London."

He seemed thoughtful for a moment. "So, Tam and Hallie will be the king and queen of London."

"That's okay, isn't it?"

I searched his face for his true feelings.

"Yeah. I'm pleased for them," he said. "Since meeting you, I came to realise that none of the business matters to me. It just doesn't. All I want is you, and now our baby, too."

"And a quiet place to live."

"That, too."

We stared at each other for a moment, and then he lifted his hand and touched my cheek with the backs of his fingers. My gaze flicked down to his generous lips, and my own parted, and I sipped a breath.

It was enough to give him permission, and he leaned in and pressed his mouth to mine. Instantly, I melted and wrapped my arms around his neck, kissing him deeper. Our tongues met and slid across one another, but this wasn't the type of hungry, frantic kiss I was used to with him. This was careful and tentative, as though we were meeting again for the first time.

I held on to a fragile hope that everything would be okay. Would Jay really be able to leave this life behind? Could he cope with a quiet one—though it wouldn't be so quiet after the baby arrived.

He hadn't doubted me for a second. He hadn't questioned the paternity of the baby or asked what I planned to do about it. He knew this was his baby and that we both wanted it, no questions asked.

As much as I wanted to carry on kissing him, we still weren't done with the talking. I wasn't the only one who needed to do some forgiving. My crime was nowhere near as serious as his, but that didn't mean it wasn't something that needed to be told.

I broke off the kiss, but we didn't part by much. He pressed his forehead to mine, our noses brushing.

I drew a breath and blurted, "I have something else I need to tell you."

He was so accepting of me—he didn't even flinch. "Anything."

"The night you rescued me from those men, I wasn't out to have a good time at a nightclub. I was there meeting someone."

Jay leaned away from me slightly and frowned. "A man?"

I shook my head. "No, a woman."

He raised an eyebrow, and I quirked the corner of my lips in a smile.

"Not like that," I chided. I hated that he could still tease a smile from me, even after everything. Guilt swamped me just for daring to smile. I shouldn't be happy with my brother's murderer.

I shouldn't be having a baby with my brother's murderer.

I hurried on with my confession. "Her name was Orla McGuinty."

He looked at me blankly.

"She was seeing Harvey Cornell behind Hallie's back."

Jay shook his head slightly, as though trying to shake into place this change of conversation. "Behind Hallie's back? You mean, before they were due to get married?"

"Exactly. They were pretty serious—or at least she thought they were—but then Harvey still continued with the wedding. She was the person who'd arranged to have Harvey Cornell shot at his wedding. She's one of the travellers."

"The Irish?"

"Yeah. She begged Harvey not to go through with the wedding, and I think he promised her it was never going to happen, but then, of course, it did. She hired the men who slipped into the wedding and paid them to shoot him, or it might not have been directly her, but someone in her family."

"Jesus." He ran his hand across his face. "So it was never about the alliance or turf wars over London?"

"No, never." I gave a sad smile. "It was simply a broken heart."

"Most people might write a diary or go out and get drunk. They wouldn't order a hit."

"You know what the travellers can be like. Even the women."

Jay's tongue flicked across his lower lip. "How did you find out?"

"I'd seen them together not long before the wedding, and I had my suspicions. Orla saw me as an enemy of the Cornells and Wynters because of my surname, and she admitted what had happened."

Jay considered what I'd told him, but I wasn't done.

"That's not the only thing," I said.

"What?"

"When I found out who was responsible, I left the Cornells notes telling them someone out there knew what had happened. It was my way of letting the Irish know that if they tried to come after the Gilligans, I would let the Cornells know the truth."

"You left those notes? I remember Leo saying he'd seen you on their territory shortly before they got the last one."

"Yeah, that was me."

"So why didn't you just tell them?"

I let out a sigh. "Orla McGuinty begged me not to let them know. I guess I was testing the water as well, seeing how Tam and Leo would react, but also warning the Irish that someone knew the truth and would be willing to spill it if they put a foot wrong. Besides, I'm a Gilligan. The Cornells and Wynters hate the Gilligans. Tam would have thought I was lying to keep the heat off his family. I had to stay anonymous."

Jay had the good sense not to ask if I was.

He pulled away from me slightly. "If the Irish all knew that they were the ones responsible for Harvey's death, and they watched on and saw that we were blaming the Gilligans, maybe it gave them the idea that continuing to drive that wedge would be a good thing."

"You mean the bomb," I said. "I don't know for sure it was them, but I never got any hint that we were the ones who set that bomb. If it wasn't us, who does that leave?"

"I was given the name of Doyle," he mused. "Tam said he might have a lead on it. I wonder if that lead is pointing in the same direction."

"Sounds like an Irish name to me."

He nodded. "I agree. I guess I might have been looking in the wrong place all this time. I'm sorry for blaming your family, Ivy."

The mention of my family still felt like a knife through my heart.

"I'm sorry," he said again.

I blinked back tears and nodded. "I don't want to talk about this anymore. I know we'll have to, but not right now, okay?"

He touched my face. "No more talking."

Chapter Twenty-Four
Jayden

Ivy was here. In my penthouse. And she was pregnant.

It felt wrong to even consider that I might be happy, especially after what I'd done. Ivy was grieving, and now she was pregnant. Pregnant. I couldn't even imagine what she must be going through emotionally right now, but I'd be there for her, no matter what. Even when she pushed me away. Maybe *especially* when she pushed me away.

A crazy amount of information had hit me. I was still processing it.

I had no doubt in my mind that I wanted this baby. It wasn't going to be easy—Ivy and I had a lot of work to do on where we'd go from here—but there was no way I wasn't going to let this work.

I wanted to scoop her up and run far away from the city with her. We'd find a little house in the countryside and get a dog.

I tucked her hair behind her ear. "Thank you for telling me, Ivy. I don't deserve you. I know that."

"You're not angry with me for not telling you sooner?"

"How could I ever be angry with you?"

I kissed her again, gently, seeking her permission.

"You're so brave, Ivy, baby. You're the bravest person I know."

I couldn't even imagine the emotional strength it was taking her to be here with me.

I kissed the tears from her cheeks and realised she wasn't the only one crying. A part of me thought she would distance herself from me, and if she had, I wouldn't have blamed her in the slightest. But she seemed as starved for me as I was for her, and she kissed me back, even through our tears.

"Not in here," she said.

I understood why. The open-plan layout of the living space meant she could see where her brother had died.

I caught her up, her thighs around my waist, and carried her into the bedroom, shutting the door behind us with my foot.

I didn't deserve her forgiveness. I didn't deserve this second chance, but I was going to grab it with both hands. I wasn't sure if I'd ever be able to make up for what I'd done to her, but I sure as hell was going to spend the rest of my life trying.

Laying her back on the bed, I covered her with my body. I kissed her mouth again, loving how she slid her tongue over mine. We'd always fit so perfectly together. I left her lip and trailed my kisses down her jaw and throat. She tasted like coming home.

"Even if you choose to punish me every day for what I did, I'll be here for it," I told her. "I'll get down on my knees and take it again and again, because no other punishment comes close to not having you in my life."

"My heart is broken, Jay. I still don't know how to mend it."

"I know. I'm so sorry, baby. Let me try. Please, just let me try."

She pressed her lips together and nodded, her eyes slipping shut as though a part of her still couldn't bear to look at me. I hated that I'd caused her such pain. It was the reason I'd been out picking fights every other night, so I could be punished.

I felt her pain as though it was my own, as though we shared one heart. But I could never fully know what she was going through, and I wouldn't insult her by claiming I did.

Carefully, as though she might break, I undressed her, pulling her t-shirt over her head, easing her sweatpants down over her hips. I reached beneath her back to unclip her bra and tossed it away.

I wanted to consume her completely, to meld myself so tightly to her that we became one person.

I took in the subtle but definite changes in her body. Her breasts were fuller than before, a light spiderweb of veins beneath the soft skin, her nipples plump and beautiful.

"Are they sensitive? I asked her. "Do they hurt?"

Tentatively, I flicked her right nipple with my tongue. It hardened, and she groaned with pleasure.

"No, just tender."

"I can't wait until your tits are swollen and full of milk." I covered her nipple fully with my mouth and sucked the hardened bud to the roof. I imagined her releasing her sweet milk to me, the taste flooding my tongue, and my cock hardened. Fuck. She was going to be so sexy as a pregnant woman and nursing mother.

I couldn't wait.

I cupped her breast, careful not to hurt her as I continued to suck. She arched beneath me. I moved to her other breast and gave it the same attention. I slid my hand across her stomach, feeling for the slight swell that signified her pregnancy. She was still early on, and to me her belly felt as flat as ever, but I looked forward to experiencing the change in her, to watching her stomach grow round and her breasts heavy. I went lower still, slipping my fingers beneath the waistband of her underwear, across the mound of her mons, and then between her folds.

"I love how you're always so wet for me."

She sighed and sank back as I dipped a finger inside her, pulling it out and tasting her. I positioned myself between her legs, ridding her of her underwear, and then ducked my head to kiss her belly.

To think she had a part of me growing inside her. I knew it was just biology, but to me it felt like a miracle.

I moved lower, spreading her legs to open her up to me. Then I lowered my mouth to her pussy and used my tongue to lick her with long, firm strokes, pausing at her clit to circle and lap before sliding back down. The tension in her stomach and thighs built, her muscles taut. Her breathing grew ragged, and I lifted my eyes to watch her expression and the way her swollen breasts bounced each time I thrust my tongue inside her.

I sensed her reach her peak and focused on her clit, licking her fast and firm, and I pushed my finger back inside her. I didn't know how much the pregnancy had increased her sensitivity, but from the noises she was making, it was a lot. She tensed beneath me, like the bow of a violin, and then shattered. My cock grew even harder at her cries, and I was desperate to be inside her, but this wasn't about me now, it was all her.

I continued to lick and suck her as she trembled through her orgasm.

"You came so beautifully for me, Ivy," I told her, moving back up her body to sweep her hair from her face. "I love seeing you like this. You're going to give us the most precious baby, do you know that?"

Her eyes fluttered open and met mine. "I missed you so much."

"I know, baby. Me, too."

She rolled towards me to kiss me. I pushed my tongue between her lips, the idea that she tasted herself on me turning me on even more.

Her hand found my cock under my clothes, and she quickly worked my belt and zipper, freeing me. I didn't want any clothing between us, so I kicked off my jeans and yanked my t-shirt over my head. Her fingers surrounded my length, squeezing me with just the right amount of pressure. She pumped her hand back and forth, swiping across the head with her thumb.

"I want you inside me," she said.

"Are you sure that's okay?"

She gave me a smile, and I loved the sight of it. "You might have a big cock, Jay, but I promise it's not long enough to penetrate my womb."

I smiled back and watched as her hand rolled up from the base to the tip. We both knew I didn't have any issues in the size department.

Even though she was already pregnant, I still wanted to fill her with my cum. That urge still hadn't left me, and I doubted it ever would. I loved knowing that my orgasm had been gifted to her in a very real sense. That I'd passed something of myself over to her in my moment of bliss, and that she now held it inside her. It was like laying my claim to her.

She was mine. She would always be mine. And I would never again do anything that would hurt her.

She pushed me back on the bed and climbed on top of me, straddling my hips. She lifted herself enough that my cock touched her entrance. Then she sank down onto me, encasing my cock in her soft, tight heat.

My eyes rolled with pleasure. "God, baby. That feels so good."

Ivy's lips parted as she circled her hips. "I don't ever want us to be apart again."

"Me neither. It's just us now. Us and our baby against the world."

I grabbed her thighs, my fingers digging into her firm flesh. She rose, slowly at first, so I could feel her sliding up every inch of my cock, before sinking back down. Her movements gradually increased in pace, and I bucked my hips to meet her.

In this position, I got to pay full attention to her beautiful tits, the way they bounced in time with her movements. Fuck, she was perfect.

I released her thigh to touch her clit, rubbing her firmly with my thumb. Her pussy was even plumper than normal, her clit swollen with blood flow. I didn't know if it was the result of her pregnancy or the orgasm she'd just had, but I liked it.

She lowered her torso over mine, her breasts pressing to my chest, and kissed me, hard and frantic. Our breath mingled, inhaling each other in. Our bodies slammed together, faster and faster as we both chased our orgasm.

Tension and heat pooled and gathered, and I knew I wouldn't be able to hold on much longer.

"Fuck. Aah, fuck, Ivy," I gasped. "Don't stop."

"I'm close, I'm close."

Her pussy clenched around my cock, and she jammed her hips down hard on mine, at the exact moment I spilled inside her. Energy poured from me into her. She squeezed me tight, rocking her hips, as though she was trying to get every last drop out of me. God, that felt incredible.

"I love you." She fell into my arms, breathing hard. "I love you so much."

"I love you, too, Jay."

I held her tight, her cheek resting against my rising and falling chest, and buried my nose in her hair.

For the first time in a month, I slept without being beaten and drunk.

Chapter Twenty-Five
Ivy

I couldn't pretend that I wasn't feeling happier now I was back in Jay's arms. That he'd been excited about my pregnancy had also eased some of the tension I'd been in the grip of over the past month.

Things still weren't going to be easy sailing, though. I hadn't married my hatred of what he'd done with my love for him, but I knew I wasn't going to be able to live without him, especially now I had his baby inside me.

But if my family had been against our relationship before, I didn't want to think what their reaction was going to be now. Them finding out had led to my brother's death, so what would they do when they found out I was carrying Jayden's baby? Were more people destined to die?

We needed to get out of London. It was the only way we were going to survive as a family.

I was also worried about what Jayden would do about the Irish now. Their gang might not have the sort of structure or money our families had, but that didn't mean they weren't dangerous. The fact they'd manged to kill off a Cornell and possibly a Wynter should be enough to prove that. I didn't want Jayden rushing over there, all guns blazing, to take his revenge.

Right now, he seemed more distracted by me than the Irish, and I hoped I could keep it that way.

Jay slept with his hand on my stomach, and I covered the back of it with my palm. My touch stirred him, and he blinked open his eyes and stared at me.

"What?" I said.

"You're still here."

"Of course I am."

"I had the horrible feeling I'd dreamed it all and I was going to wake up and you were gone."

I smiled. "I'm not going anywhere."

He pulled me against him and gave me one of those full-bodied hugs that made my heart swell with joy. I buried my nose against his skin and closed my eyes, unable to believe I had him back.

"When can we leave?" I asked him. "We need to get out of the city."

He pressed his lips together, and his gaze darted away. My heart sank. I already knew what was coming.

"There's just one thing I have to deal with before we can go."

"Jayden, no."

"I have to warn Tam about the Irish. They killed his brother at the altar and potentially set that bomb. Tam has a right to know about the threat. Hallie, too. What if I did nothing and something happened to Hallie or my niece? You said before, no more killing."

"And what if you get hurt? I couldn't handle that, not now."

"One last job, and then I'm done, I swear it."

I closed my eyes, going over my options. I could emotionally blackmail him right now. I could tell him that if he wanted me and the baby in his life, he needed to choose me now, but I also couldn't do that to him. I knew he was right. If he decided—or I forced him—not to care about his sister and baby niece, what kind of man would that make him? Not one I wanted to have watching over me and our baby.

Jay tried again. "You don't want Tam to keep believing your family are responsible for Harvey's death and the bombing, do you?"

"Will it make any difference? He's already pushing my family out of the city."

"I know." He bit his lower lip. "I helped him in that."

"You did?"

"Yes, when I thought they were responsible for the bomb, I put plans in place. If you'd told me sooner, Ivy, maybe I wouldn't have needed to."

I exhaled long and deep. "We've both done wrong."

Jay squeezed my hand.

"I want you to come with me and meet Tam and tell him what you know."

I widened my eyes. "No, Jay. I can't."

"You can. What is it you're afraid of? You weren't the one who killed Harvey."

Shame filled me. "No, but I left those notes. I could have just come out and told him the truth about what happened to his brother. I know how that feels now, but I didn't before. I understand the sort of pain both Tam and Leo must have been going through, and they never knew who was responsible. I could have done something to help that, just a little, and I didn't."

He held my gaze with his. "Ivy, I'm not going to make you do anything you don't want to, but now that I have you back,

I also don't want to let you out of my sight for a second." His hand tightened around mine. "You know there are people who aren't going to be happy about this."

I nodded. "I know."

"Tam will be fine, I promise," he reassured me. "He's not as much of an arsehole as he makes out."

I managed a smile. "You sure about that?"

"Yeah. Hallie and the baby have softened him."

"You think that'll be the same with you?"

"Ivy, you've already softened me. I'm like a giant marshmallow now you're in my life."

To my surprise, I found myself laughing. Instantly, a wave of guilt swept over me, and my eyes filled with tears. How could I laugh with the man who'd killed my brother?

This wasn't going to be easy. None of this was going to be easy.

We showered together, and rediscovered each other's bodies under the water, and then dressed.

We took Jayden's Range Rover—no more bike riding for me from now on—and he drove us to Tam and Hallie's house.

The Cornells' property was even more impressive than my father's. Double iron gates that opened electronically. A wide gravel driveway. A double-fronted, detached home. A jab of something akin to jealousy—or perhaps it was longing—went through me. They had a gorgeous home.

Jay parked on the gravel in front of the house, and we both climbed out.

I felt horribly self-conscious. How much did Tam know about what had happened? What about Hallie? Would she be protective of her brother?

A beautiful woman I recognised to be Hallie Cornell moved forward to greet me. She looked tired, which was unsurprising considering what she'd been through at her baby's birth, plus she had a newborn. Her clothes were baggy—probably to hide any excess baby weight—but she was still stunning.

I froze in place, unsure what she intended to do when she reached me. Would she slap me or push me away? Did she plan to scream at me and tell me to stay away from her brother?

"Ivy," she said, her eyes full of sympathy. "I'm so sorry."

To my surprise, she opened her arms and pulled me into a hug. Hallie held me tight, in the kind of hug I'd expect from someone I was close to, not someone I barely knew. The tears that were always so close to the surface these days sprang to my eyes, and I found myself choking back a sob.

Jayden had clearly already filled them in on what had happened, and also the nature of our relationship. I wondered how much they'd warned him off me, initially. I assumed they had—I would have, if the situation had been reversed. But then this family was used to love springing from the most surprising of places, so perhaps they understood and empathised far more than I'd given them credit for.

She released me, and Tam stepped forwards.

He didn't hug me, and for that I was grateful. There was still something incredibly intimidating about Tam Cornell. Even now, his expression was serious.

"I'm so sorry things were pushed to such a terrible situation," he said. "I know how it is to lose a brother."

I ducked my head in a nod. "Thank you."

Were they going to be so kind to me after they discovered the secret I'd been keeping from them? I'd grown up being told practically every day that the Wynters and Cornells were bad people, but I was quickly learning that wasn't the case at all.

I clung tighter to Jayden's hand. No matter what he'd said to me about how he felt, there was still that fear he'd choose his family over me if it came down to it. If Tam told him that it was me or them, which way would Jay go?

My heart told me he'd choose me, but still that niggling fear remained in my head. If Jay didn't want me, and my family continued to ostracise me because of my relationship with him and what it had resulted in, then I'd end up alone and pregnant.

The other brother, Leo, was also here with Kaja, standing in the open doorway of the house. They seemed happy together, her standing in front of him, so her back was to his chest. He had his arms over both her shoulders, and his chin rested on the top of her head. They seemed easy and comfortable together, though from what Jay had told me, things hadn't started out that way. Kaja had walked away from her family, too, to be with Leo. I didn't know the exact details, but I was aware that some bad shit had gone down and people were hurt.

Was that just how it was with our lives?

Jay cleared his throat. "We're here to talk to you about something...a few things, actually."

Tam's gaze flicked between us. "That sound ominous."

"It's not," Jay reassured him. "Some of it is good news. The rest...well, you'll have to decide what you want to do with the information."

"You'd better come inside."

We followed them into the house and through to the huge living room. Everyone found a seat, and I perched on one of the cream leather sofas next to Jay, my hands clasped in my lap. My stomach roiled with nerves, and nausea swelled beneath. I couldn't tell if it was a bout of morning sickness or caused by the adrenaline.

"Shall we start with the good news?" Hallie suggested.

Jay cleared his throat. "Ivy's pregnant."

My cheeks flushed hot. Would they think I was stupid for getting myself knocked up by someone who should have been my enemy? Maybe I was—young, stupid, and naïve—but that didn't make me want this baby and everything that came with it any the less. Being young didn't automatically make someone a bad mother. And anyway, it wasn't as though I was much younger than Hallie, and no one judged her, did they?

Hallie clapped both her hands to her mouth and squealed. "Oh my God. That's amazing. I'm going to be an auntie? Baby Madeline is going to have a cousin? This is the best news ever."

I exchanged a glance and tentative smile with Jay. He was happy, too. I could tell.

My heart swelled with happiness, my eyes filling with tears once more. Jesus, what was wrong with me? The slightest little emotion these days, and it was like I'd sprung a leak. But then I remembered I was pregnant and I'd recently lost my brother and had almost lost the man I loved, so it was hardly surprising I was emotional.

Tam got up and shook Jay's hand. "Congratulations, mate."

"Thanks. This baby will make a man of me, I know it."

Hallie hugged her brother, then Leo and Kaja came over to say congratulations.

"Do you know when the baby is due?" Hallie asked.

I shook my head. "Not yet. I haven't had any doctor's appointments or anything."

"You need to get that sorted. There are supplements you need to be on to make sure the baby develops properly."

I smiled. "Yes, Mum."

"So, what was the other thing you needed to tell us?" Tam asked.

I shifted uncomfortably, the shot of dopamine I'd received from the baby news fading. This was the moment where everything could change. When they found out that I'd known all along who had killed Harvey, they might easily change their minds about me.

"I believe I know who killed Harvey," I said, my voice trembling. "He was seeing a girl from the traveller community right before the wedding."

Tam's eyes narrowed. "The traveller community? You mean Finbar Fury's gang?"

"That's right. She and Harvey were serious—at least, she thought they were. When he went ahead with the wedding, she was furious, and she arranged to have him shot. I guess doing it at the wedding drilled home her point."

Leo spoke up. "How do we know you're not just saying this to get your family off the hook?"

"My family have basically disowned me because of my relationship with Jay and what that's done to us. Now I'll have to tell them I'm pregnant with the baby of the man who killed Bruno. I don't know how they'll react to that, but trust me when I say it's not going to be good. You know what happened the last time. If they hadn't tried to warn Jay away from me, none of this would have happened. I'm not trying to get them off the hook."

Jay backed me up. "She's not, Leo, and she knew about this before she and I even got together. There's proof that she knew before we became a thing."

Tam's eyes narrowed. "What kind of proof?"

There was no denying that Tam Cornell was an imposing man. But I'd been around intimidating men all my life.

I straightened my spine. "You've received several notes telling you that someone knew who'd killed Harvey."

"How do you know that."

"I was the one who sent them."

Hallie frowned and angled her body towards me. "You sent those notes? Why?"

I exhaled the air in my lungs through my nose. "I was testing the water, letting the Irish know that if they tried to come after the Gilligans, I was prepared to let the Cornells know exactly what happened to Harvey. But I didn't want the girl to get in trouble, despite what she did." I wasn't going to say out loud that maybe Harvey deserved a bit of what he got, especially considering I was sitting opposite his two surviving brothers. "But I also didn't want us Gilligans to be blamed for something we never did. Same with the bombing. As far as I know, my family didn't plant that bomb."

"The name Doyle is Irish," Jay said, linking his fingers between his knees. "I believe they wanted it to look like it was the Gilligans. They wanted us to fight amongst ourselves. If we're fighting each other, no one is looking in their direction."

Tam nodded. "And that's exactly what's happened. We've made ourselves weaker because of it. When I told you that

I thought we had a lead on the name, it was also pointing towards the Irish, we just hadn't had confirmation of it. Will you tell us who the girl is?"

I shook my head. "No. I'm sorry."

I'd told Jay, but I trusted him to keep the secret.

Tam's lips pinched. "I can't imagine she's the one responsible for what happened. Finbar probably found out about the relationship and used it as an excuse to kill Harvey. The girls in the traveller community often marry young. Hearing that Harvey used one of their girls and then went on to marry someone else would have been like spitting in her face. If they were the ones to kill Harvey and set off that bomb, we can't just let them get away with it."

"If they were the ones to set the bomb," Jayden said, anger flashing in his eyes. "I want to do more than warn them off."

Tam nodded. "And then what?"

Jay glanced over at me. "Then Ivy and I are leaving London."

Around the room, mouths dropped open.

"No, you can't," Hallie cried. "This is your home."

Jay took my hand and squeezed it. "It's not safe for us here. We don't want to raise this baby looking over our shoulders the whole time."

"You think Greyson Gilligan will come after you?" Leo asked.

"I think they'll do everything they can to tear us apart."

"Then it's the Gilligans who'll need to leave, not you." Tam glanced at me. "Sorry, Ivy."

I didn't know what to say. My chest ached because I was losing my family, but what could I do? They'd chosen their hatred of Jayden over their love for me. If Bruno had simply accepted our relationship and not gone to threaten Jay, he would still be alive today.

My family blamed me for my part in what had happened without ever bothering to look at themselves.

Chapter Twenty-Six
Jayden

"I don't want you to go," Ivy said, kissing me again.

"I know. I'm sorry."

I felt like I was forever saying sorry to her. I'd do my best, once this was taken care of, to never do anything I'd have to apologise to her for again.

I kissed her hard, then pressed my forehead to hers. "Take care of the little bean while I'm gone."

I put my hand to her flat belly, and she covered it with her palm.

She nodded, and her chin trembled. My beautiful girl. She'd been through so much already, and my heart tugged to give her what she wanted and stay, but this was the man who'd killed my father. While I'd been raging at the Gilligans, he'd been sitting back and laughing at the shitstorm he'd stirred up.

The head of the Irish, Finbar Fury, was a mad bastard, and everyone knew it. He was the type of bloke who would tear someone's ear off in a bar fight just 'cause he thought the person had been looking at him the wrong way.

Had Finbar wanted my father dead all along, or had Tam and Leo been the target? I had to wonder. After all, they'd been the ones to sneak onto the traveller site and kill the Estonian responsible for murdering Leo's fiancée, amongst other things. Tam and Leo had torched one of the traveller's cars, but it was doubtful the Irish were bothered about that—it was probably nicked anyway. It was more that the Estonians had been under their protection and the Cornells had dared come onto their territory.

They'd killed Harvey because of the girl, but I assumed the bombing had also been in part revenge for Tam and Leo attacking their camp.

"Time to go," Tam said.

Similar farewells had been going on between him and Hallie, and Leo and Kaja, too. Maybe it was old-fashioned for the men to go off fighting while the women stayed home with the babies, but we weren't the type of men who'd allow their women to put themselves in danger. If something was heavy, we carried it. If something was dirty, we dealt with it. If there was danger, we put ourselves in the way of it. That was just how it was.

I hugged Ivy one last time, both of us clinging to one another, and then forced myself to let go. Unable to make eye contact with her again for fear that I'd break and refuse to leave her side, I put my head down and followed Tam out to where the vehicles were parked. We were taking Tam's classic-style Land Rover, which though brand-new, had the style of a military vehicle.

I took a seat in back, while Tam drove and Leo rode shotgun.

We'd pulled together as many men as possible—from both the Wynter and Cornell sides—to meet a mile from the traveller site on the outskirts of Bexley Farm. We'd roped in almost twenty men, and while the Irish might be on home turf, we were larger in number, plus we had the element of surprise.

The Irish weren't going to know what hit them.

The longer I was allowed to dwell on it, the angrier I became. Some of the fire I'd thought had died away completely since losing Ivy returned to me. I hated the idea of Finbar Fury laughing behind our backs.

We needed to drive the travellers away from the city and show them that the Wynters and Cornells wouldn't sit by and allow our family members to be killed.

They needed to understand that we were onto them and we wouldn't stand for it.

We did the drive in near silence, not even the radio on to break things up. Mentally, we all needed to be prepared, and now was not the time for casual chit-chat, despite all the bombs I had dropped back at the house.

We were first to arrive at the meeting spot.

My stomach knotted. I'd hoped there would at least have been a few people here to meet us.

How many men would come to our call? The Irish were known to be ruthless, and that might mean some would hold back, but I hoped enough would come to ensure our victory.

Tam parked the Land Rover, and we all climbed out, slamming the doors behind us. From the tense atmosphere that settled over us all, I got the feeling Tam had been expecting people to already be here, too.

I didn't bother saying anything to try to reassure him. Right now, my words were meaningless.

The grumble of an engine approaching, followed by the roar of a couple of motorbikes, met my ears.

Our call had been heard.

Over the next thirty minutes, more men arrived, all of them prepared and ready for a fight. We shook their hands and clapped them on the back. The atmosphere morphed to one of joviality rather than war.

When it looked as though everyone was here, Tam raised his voice to get their attention.

"Thanks for coming, everyone. It seemed we have a scourge on our city, one we'd been too preoccupied to notice. We've recently learned Finbar Fury and his gang were responsible for my brother, Harvey's, murder, and we also believe them responsible for the bomb that killed Marlon Wynter."

He was like a sergeant instructing his army.

"I don't want any women or children harmed," Tam instructed us. "I mean it. No shooting unless you know exactly who you're shooting at—got it?"

The caravans were like tin cans. Bullets could easily penetrate them and kill whoever was inside. Accidents happened that way, and none of us were into taking the lives of innocents.

"Our main sights are on Finbar Fury. Even if he wasn't directly behind Harvey's shooting, nothing goes down among his people without him knowing about it. I'd like to hear the truth come directly from Finbar's mouth, so ideally I want him taken alive, but if we have to kill him, so be it."

Everyone nodded in agreement.

"There's enough of us that we can surround the site and take them from all directions. We divided into four. No one is getting off that site without our say-so."

A roar of camaraderie rose among the group.

We split up.

Since I was the head of the Wynter Syndicate and the men who'd responded, it made sense that I lead them. We were fewer in number than the Cornells, but I knew his men were ruthless and loyal. Together, we skirted the edges of Bexley Farm, staying well behind the line of trees so as to remain hidden. We needed this attack to be a surprise.

We remained out of view, our weapons held at our sides, until the time hit the hour.

"Now," I told them.

We slipped out between the trees, jogged the short distance to the edge of the farm, and drew to a halt.

I stared down over the empty field.

There was clear evidence that the travellers been here until recently. Rectangles of brown grass against the green, discoloured from lack of sunlight, marked the spots where the caravans had been sitting for months on end. Bulging black bin bags were scattered across the area, together with plenty of rubbish that hadn't been thrown away. A burnt-out car sat at the far end—a blackened hulk of metal, the glass missing from the windows.

I shook my head. "Well, fuck."

A thought occurred to me, and I spun around, aiming my gun, suddenly certain this was some kind of trick and the Irish would attack from behind. No one was there.

"Don't think there's going to be any fucking fighting," one of my men grumbled.

"Only if we want to fight between ourselves," another replied.

From the shouts across the other side of the field, it was clear Tam and Leo had come to the same conclusion.

"Come on," I told them. "No point in hanging out here."

We retreated back to where we'd left the vehicles and met up with the others.

"Did they hear we were coming?" Tam said, his face like thunder.

I shook my head. "Even if they had, it takes time to mobilise an entire camp of people. They'd never have got away without us seeing them."

"Fuck. Now what?"

"We keep our ear to the ground. They're bound to show up somewhere."

Tam shook his head. "I'm concerned what their plan is."

"If they have one." I licked my lower lip. "I guess we'll find out soon enough."

"They're travellers," Leo said. "Maybe they just got itchy feet and decided to move on. It might not have anything to do with us."

It was a possibility. I knew one thing for sure—I wasn't going to charge all over the country looking for them.

"They're away from London," I said. "That was our plan, to move them on, and they've moved. Maybe we just need to take it as someone smiling down on us for once and go the fuck home."

Tam put his hands on his hips. "Okay, but I'm not sure we've seen the last of Finbar and his gang."

I didn't care.

All I wanted was to be back with Ivy. I'd done my duty as far as supporting the Cornells and watching out for my sister went. My conscience, for this part at least, was clear.

Chapter Twenty-Seven

Ivy

Months had passed and we should have left the city already.

I knew that, but the love and warmth of the Cornell-Wynter household had caught me in its grasp. I'd never really had girlfriends before, but now I had Hallie and Kaja, and even Hallie's friend, Layla, had welcomed me into the fold. I loved being around baby Madeline, too, feeling as though I was getting some practice in before our baby arrived. If Jayden and I ever married—which I was pretty sure was in the cards—it meant Madeline would be my niece, too, even if it wasn't by blood, and I loved the thought of our baby and Maddie being able to grow up together.

My father and brother hadn't so much as called me, and I was grateful they'd left me alone. I didn't know how long it would last, though.

I was sitting in the Cornells' kitchen, drinking decaf tea with the others, when my phone rang.

It was Mara.

"Your father and brother have been here, wanting to know where you are."

"What did you tell them?"

"What could I say, Ivy? I had to tell them you weren't staying here currently. You know I couldn't lie to them. They'd find out the truth eventually."

"It's okay, Mara. I wouldn't expect you to lie on my behalf." If she'd lied and my father found out, he'd take his anger out on her, and I would never want that.

"I thought you were going to get out of the city?" she said.

I exhaled a breath through my nose. "We were. We are. I don't know. The Cornells don't think we should be the ones to leave."

I didn't say how I was starting to feel the same. How I'd been welcomed into their growing family with open arms and spent days talking with Hallie about all things to do with babies.

Besides, I still had my degree to finish. How was I going to do that if I left London? And I didn't want Jayden to have to give up everything for me. Perhaps people could argue that I'd given up everything for him, but it had been my family who'd been behind that.

There were still times when I had to push my thoughts of what Jayden had done to the farthest corners of my mind to prevent myself spiralling into grief and depression, and I imagined it was something I'd end up needing some serious therapy for in the years to come, but time had started to heal my heart, and Jayden's constant adoration and support had helped that.

"You can stay in the house as long as you want, Mara. I don't want you out of a job or a place to live. It's yours as long as you want it."

"That's kind of you, Ivy, but I'm not sure your father and brother will feel that way."

"It's my house. It's my name on the deeds."

Her voice was quiet. "Yes, I know."

She didn't have to say what she was thinking out loud. We both already knew it. If I was not there, then my father and brother would likely physically force Mara out of the house and not care where she ended up. After all, they'd shown their complete lack of respect for my privacy when they'd tossed the house in search of Jayden's key. My father believed that anything the family owned automatically belonged to him first, no matter whose name was on the deeds.

"I'll need some help after the baby's born," I said. "I have no idea how I'm going to cope."

That wasn't strictly true. Hallie was giving me all the tips she'd learned since having her own baby. But, like me, without a mother or any sisters to help her, Hallie had been learning on the job.

I lowered my hand to the swell of my belly. I was still only twenty weeks along—just halfway—but my pregnancy was obvious now. That I was short and curvy probably didn't help matters. If I was one of those tall, lean women, I'd probably barely have a bump, but it was like my entire body decided it was going to get round—not just my belly. Not that Jay seemed to mind. He loved my swollen body and couldn't get enough of it. It had never occurred to me that a man might find his partner's pregnancy a turn-on—I'd always thought it would go the other way and they'd somehow be disgusted or worried about hurting the baby—but each extra pound only seemed to make Jay want me even more. He was completely obsessed with my growing breasts, and I genuinely wondered if our baby would have to compete with him for boob time.

"I'm sure you'll cope just fine," Mara said. "But if you decide you need help, I'll be here for you."

"Thanks, Mara."

I wondered how Jayden would feel about having a live-in nanny who was once on my father's payroll?

We ended the call, and I checked the time. I was meeting Jayden at the hospital, and a flood of nerves combined with excitement went through me. I squeezed myself in a secret hug. We were finding out about the sex of the baby today. Neither of us had wanted to wait, and it just seemed more practical to know if we were having a boy or a girl.

I said goodbye to Hallie and Kaja and left the house with them bidding me good luck and making me promise to call and let them know the result as soon as possible. I thought they were almost as excited as I was. I drove one of the four-by-fours to the hospital, found a parking spot, paid the extortionate charge, and then went to meet Jayden by the front entrance.

He was already there, and my heart surged with love and pride that he was there, waiting for me. I noted how everyone glanced in his direction, and when he scooped me around the waist and pressed his lips to mine for a kiss, I practically felt myself glowing with happiness.

"You ready to find out?" he asked.

"I can't wait."

We made our way to the maternity unit, registered with the sonographer, and took a seat. Within fifteen minutes, we were called in. I kept a tight hold of Jayden's hand as we went into the room and was greeted by the sonographer.

"Twenty-week scan," she said.

I nodded. "That's right."

"Great. Hop up on here for me." She patted the padded gurney.

I lay on the hospital bed, my top rolled up and stretchy maternity jeans pulled down. Cold gel was smoothed onto my stomach. I prayed everything would be all right with the baby. After going through so much already, I felt like we deserved this little bit of happiness.

"Do you want to know what you're having?"

Jayden and I glanced at each other, and I nodded. "Yes, please."

The sonographer moved the wand around. "Let's have a look then." She pointed out the baby's spine, the hands and feet and head. "Aah, there we go. It's never one hundred percent, but I'd say you're having a little boy."

"A boy?" I blinked back tears and locked on to Jayden's loving gaze. "You're going to have a son."

He leaned down and kissed me. "*We're* going to have a son. I can't believe how happy you've made me, Ivy. I'm the luckiest man alive."

The sonographer printed out some pictures for us, and we left the hospital with me barely watching where I was going. I couldn't take my eyes off the fuzzy black-and-white photographs. This baby was really happening. A boy. He was real to me now, not just a swell of my belly or tender breasts. There was actually another little person growing inside me. I felt like I wanted to tell everyone I passed so they were aware of this miracle.

"I'll walk you to your car," he told me.

We crossed the car park hand in hand. But as we reached where I'd parked, Jayden pulled me to an abrupt halt. I'd still been staring at the pictures and hadn't looked up.

"Hello, Ivy."

I froze. My father's voice.

With a rock in my gut, I lifted my eyes to where my father stood beside my vehicle.

I glanced down at the gun in his hand.

He stared at my stomach. "The rumours are true then? You're pregnant with this fucker's baby? How could you? How could you betray the family like that?"

"Dad, please, don't."

"Don't what?"

"Don't do whatever it is you're planning."

He raised the gun and pointed it at Jayden. "You mean getting rid of this piece of scum, once and for all."

"No!" I jumped in front of Jay. "I won't let you. No more killing."

"Ivy," Jayden said, a warning in his tone. "What the fuck are you doing?"

"What does it look like? I won't let him hurt you."

My father's jaw tensed. "Get out of the way," he spat.

I held out both arms, making myself bigger. "No, never. You're not going to do this."

He scowled. "Jesus, Ivy. Move out of the fucking way."

"So you can shoot Jayden in broad daylight in the middle of London? What are you thinking? All that's going to happen here is you're going to prison."

He scoffed. "People like us don't go to prison."

From over my shoulder, Jay said, "Move out of the way, Ivy."

"No, Jayden. Never."

"I won't let my pregnant girlfriend put herself between me and a bullet."

There was craziness in my father's eyes, and I didn't trust that he wouldn't shoot me just to get to him. But I wasn't just going to let him kill Jayden.

"This is your grandbaby," I told my father, risking lowering one hand to cover my belly. "Are you really going to shoot your own daughter and kill your unborn grandchild?"

"No, because you're going to get out of the fucking way, but if I had to put an end to that…thing…growing inside you, then I would. If you think I want to be related by blood to the bastard who murdered my son, then you can think again."

I couldn't believe it had come to this. "And you'd murder your own daughter in cold blood to make that happen?"

Jayden's hands were on my shoulders, his fingers tightening almost imperceptibly, and I knew he was going to try to move me out of the way. I braced my feet on the ground, but he was far bigger and stronger than me. If he moved me, he was dead, I knew it.

"Jay, no, please. Don't do it."

"I love you, Ivy. You and our baby son."

He hauled me to one side, hard enough to make me stumble. I didn't want to fall, aware of the possibility of any impact harming the baby, and pinwheeled my arms to keep to my feet.

Behind me, the crack of a gunshot went off, followed swiftly by a second.

I spun around and screamed.

Epilogue: Nine Months Later

Ivy

I stood outside the door of the wood-panelled Council Chamber at Hackney Town Hall and sucked in a breath. I shouldn't be nervous, but I was. Today was a life-changing day, and though I wanted it more than anything, I was uncomfortable putting myself on display in front of all those people.

I knew I'd feel better when I was back at his side—I always did.

We didn't have many guests coming, and that was fine by me. I'd never been someone who'd dreamed of my wedding day, and now it was here, I was simply grateful we were here at all.

Memories of that day in the hospital car park came back to me.

My father's bullet had only skimmed Jay's arm, and somehow Jayden had managed to wrestle the gun off my father. The second shot had been Jay pulling the trigger, and my father had taken the bullet.

It had hit his hip, shattering the bone. He'd needed to have a hip replacement, something that he never would have been happy about—an operation he considered to be for old people—and the procedure had weakened him. While he was in the hospital, he'd ended up with sepsis, and it had almost killed him.

He was living in assisted care now down on the Dorset Coast. Despite what he'd done, it was the best money could buy.

The police had asked questions, of course, but those we had on our books had interfered with evidence and, in the end, a private word with the judge had the case thrown out of court.

Aiden had done the sensible thing and left; I wasn't sure where to. I believed he may have gone abroad to start again. It was clear my family no longer had any standing in the city.

The doors opened, and Hallie's head popped out. "Ready?"

I swallowed hard. "Ready."

Music played, and I forced my feet to move.

We hadn't gone for the traditional roles of having a best man or bridesmaids. Since it wasn't as though my father could give me away, I hadn't been able to entertain the thought of the rest of it either. Jay understood completely and supported my decision. As he'd pointed out, it wasn't as though we'd done anything else the traditional way either. It was our wedding, and no one else mattered.

That still didn't stop me missing the people who should have filled the empty seats, however, and the man who should have been giving me away. I would always carry this pain inside of me. I just needed to figure out how to live with it.

My new family definitely went some way to healing that pain.

I walked down the short aisle of the registry office, smiling self-consciously. Despite my protests about not wanting to do things traditionally—and clearly I was nowhere near a virgin—I'd still gone for the white dress. It had a boned bodice, my shoulders left bare. My hair was caught up in a French knot with white baby's breath flowers woven through it. There was a fishtail train—simple but elegant.

I hadn't wanted us to marry while I was pregnant, despite Jay's insistence that I was still beautiful. I felt like an absolute whale, and I didn't want the photographs I hoped to cherish for the rest of my life to be of me looking like a beach ball draped in a tablecloth.

Jayden stood at the front of the room in a dark-grey suit, a clove-red carnation in his lapel. We locked eyes, and I found myself choking back tears again. God, he was so gorgeous, I couldn't believe he was mine. Even though I wasn't pregnant anymore, I still hadn't managed to shift the crying habit.

I reached him, and he pulled me in and kissed me.

"You're supposed to wait until the 'I do,'" Leo shouted from the audience.

A few people laughed and clapped.

Jay leaned in and spoke against my ear.

"It was worth the wait," he said. "You look incredible."

I beamed. I felt incredible, too. I'd worked hard to get my figure back over the past few months, though I knew my body would never be quite the same as it had been before. It didn't matter, though. Jay seemed to want me just as much as ever, and I'd happily take a rounder stomach and a few stretch marks if it meant I got to have a family of my own.

The celebrant started the service, and I held Jay's hand as I twisted slightly to cast my gaze over the congregation. So many faces smiled back at me—Mara, holding our baby boy in her arms. Hallie, with her daughter, Madeline. Leo and Kaja sat side by side—they were both teased all the time that they would be next. Some of the friends I'd made from university were here, too. My heart still ached for Bruno and my family. I wished more than anything that things could have been different, but that wasn't the case.

Sometimes we didn't always get everything we wanted.

I'd always felt like an outcast, even among my own family, but here, with these people, I'd finally found my place.

Tam's father had recently announced he was retiring, and so Tam would be at the head of the Cornell-Wynter syndicate. I'd been surprised that Jay had given in so easily about that, but he promised me he was fine. Hallie was as much as part of the Wynters as Jayden, so the Wynter family was represented.

"Anyway," he'd told me, "I have you and the baby now. You're my responsibility, and I want us to be able to do whatever we want, whenever we want. If we decide to get that cottage in the countryside one day, then that's exactly what we'll do."

Jayden seemed more at ease with life, too. He'd always worried he'd never fully fill his father's shoes, without ever considering for a moment that maybe he didn't have to. Now he was forging his own way in the world, with us by his side.

After the service and reception, we had our honeymoon to go on. Everyone told us we should leave the baby behind, but we were a family now. Besides, he was a good sleeper, and I was still feeding him, so we wouldn't be leaving him anywhere. We'd never enjoy ourselves if we were worrying about him the whole time.

The celebrant was watching at me expectantly, and I realised the time had arrived for me to say my part.

"I do," I said, grinning at Jay. "I do, I do, I do."

***

Our stilted hut on Bora Bora overlooked the clear South Pacific ocean.

I stood on the wraparound balcony, leaning my forearms on the wooden railing, warmed by the bright sun. Beneath me, a shoal of brightly coloured fish darted through the water.

I'd been nervous about being so close to the sea, but it wasn't as though baby Arthur—Art for short—could even crawl yet, so it wasn't going to be dangerous for him. I couldn't help my protective mothering instinct from going into overdrive, though. I still saw danger everywhere, which was hardly surprising considering how the last twelve months had been.

For the moment, though, with my new husband and new baby in this beautiful place, I felt something akin to peace settle inside me.

Jayden's arms wrapped around me from behind, and he planted a kiss between my neck and shoulder.

"He's asleep," he said.

One of the things we'd liked about the hut was that it had two bedrooms. It meant we had the extra bedroom for Art, so Jay and I still had our privacy.

"Is he now?" I twisted in my husband's arms and looped mine around his neck. "What should we do now then?"

"You know what they say? Sleep when the baby's sleeping."

I arched an eyebrow. "You want to sleep?"

"I want to get you in bed, but I don't plan on getting much rest."

I giggled. "Now that's what I want to hear."

His lips captured mine, and I arched against him, pressing my breasts to his chest. He caught my hair in his fingers, knotting tightly enough to tug at my scalp with just the right amount of pressure. I let out a groan, and his hands moved from my hair, his fingers brushing down my spine to come to rest on my bottom. Our kiss grew deeper until we were grinding on each other like a couple of horny teenagers.

"If I don't get you naked in the next thirty seconds," he growled. "I'm going to lose my mind."

He scooped me into his arms and carried me back into the hut. I only had a bikini and a loose, almost see-through caftan over the top, so it literally took him seconds to get me naked. The bikini was held together with mere strings at the sides, which he only needed to pull for the entire thing to fall off. Jay just wore shorts—the only times he'd bothered to wear a shirt was when we'd been out for dinner—and his beautiful torso was already tanned a deep honeyed brown. I yanked the shorts from his hips so his cock sprang out to meet me, and he kicked them away.

We kissed again, and his tongue slid over mine, his teeth nibbling my lower lip. I sighed with pleasure against his mouth. He always felt so good, as though we both were made to fit together, one complementing the other.

I reached for his cock and wrapped my fingers around him, and he slid his hand between my thighs. I was already wet for him, and he stroked me open before pushing one finger inside and then adding a second.

I dropped my forehead to his chest, my legs almost buckling. "Oh God, Jay. That feels so good, but I want to taste you."

He slipped his fingers from me, and I fell to my knees before him, worshipping him.

He gently touched the top of my head. "I love you in this position, baby."

I wanted to please him. I wanted to make him come so hard that he'd never once regret marrying me or wonder if another woman could fuck him better.

Keeping my eyes lifted to his, I gripped his base in my fist to hold him steady and parted my lips. I slipped out my tongue and licked his slit, coating my tastebuds in his salty precum. Then I swirled around the head and covered him with my lips, sinking as deep as I could.

"Ah, fuck. That's incredible."

He knotted one of his hands in my hair and tugged on the strands, hard enough to hurt, but the sensation only sent heat pooling between my thighs. Unable to help myself, I used my other hand to rub my clit, while I bobbed back and forth on his cock.

"I love seeing you touch yourself," he said. "It's so fucking hot."

I was wet, and sucking his cock was making me wetter. His grunts and moans from above me only urged me on. I inserted my fingers inside myself, breathing hard through my nostrils as I ground down on my hand. Fuck, I wanted him inside me.

Jayden clearly felt the same way. "Ivy, stop. I'm going to come, and I want to be inside you."

I sank down deep, hitting the back of my throat, and breathed through my nose to hold back on my gag reflex. Then I slid back up, slowly, feeling every ridge and vein beneath my lips.

"Your mouth is so pretty wrapped around my cock," he praised me.

I let him pop from between my lips and gave his slit an extra lick.

"You're so good at that. Now spread those legs so I can get my dick inside you."

He helped me to my feet and pushed me onto my back on the bed. He covered me with his body and ducked his head to my chest.

My tits were swollen and heavy with milk.

He licked my nipple and, to my embarrassment, pale milk squirted from it.

"Oh my God, Jay."

He licked his lips. "Mmm, sweet."

He cupped the weight of my breast in his hand and covered the whole of my nipple with his mouth.

The heavy ache in my breasts, followed by the rush and tingle of my milk letting down, felt something close to orgasm. His fingers hooked inside me, and I grew heady with pleasure while he sucked on me. I'd never known this could be such a high. My body was filled with endorphins, and my tits seemed to have a direct connection to my pussy.

His Adam's apple bobbed as he swallowed.

"You have to stop," I told him, though I didn't want him to. "There won't be anything left for the baby."

He grinned and did as I'd asked. Neither of us would ever want to deprive Arthur of anything, no matter how good it felt.

Jay settled himself between my legs and pressed his cock to my wet slit. He rubbed the head up and down a couple of times, deliberately applying extra pressure to my sensitive clit.

I'd been worried things would be different down there and he wouldn't want me anymore, but that hadn't been a problem at all. My belly was softer now and crisscrossed with stretchmarks that still hadn't turned silvery, but he kissed them every night on his way down to suck my clit.

He grabbed both my hands and pinned them above my head and then drove into me in one movement. He was so deep, my pussy stretched around him. God, that felt good.

He lowered his head to my breast and sucked my nipple into his mouth again, rolling and grazing the hardened peak with his teeth. My milk let down once more, and he swallowed while his hips pistoned back and forth, ramming into me. The sound of our flesh slapping together filled the room, together with all the heavy breathing and groans of pleasure.

"Look at the way your tits bounce every time I fuck you," he growled. "Fuck, that's so hot."

I might have felt self-conscious if it wasn't for the heated way he stared down at me, the pure unadulterated hunger in his eyes that told me he wanted me.

"I'm going to come inside you, Ivy," he said. "I'm going to fill that sweet little cunt up with my cum. Maybe I will put another baby inside you."

I gasped for breath. "I can't get pregnant while I'm breastfeeding."

He gave a wicked smile. "I'm not sure that's true. At least, I hope it's not. I'd love to see you round with another baby while your breasts were still filled with milk."

"You're obsessed, Jay." I laughed.

"Obsessed with you and our little family. My life was so fucking empty before you came into it, and I didn't even realise."

He fucked me harder, and my orgasm built.

"Oh, fuck, Jay. Yes."

I wrapped myself around him, pulling him deeper.

We both shattered around each other, and he clamped his hand over my mouth to prevent my cries waking the baby. I tasted salt on his palm. My skin was damp, and we dropped together into a sweaty pile, happy and sated.

"There's nowhere else I'd rather be," he told me. "You know that, don't you? Your arms are my home, no matter where we end up."

I snuggled into his chest and let out a happy sigh. He was completely right.

He was my home. I'd finally found where I belonged.

Acknowledgments

Thank you, as always, to my long-time editor, Emmy Ellis. It seems I still haven't managed to shock you with my words!

Thanks to my proofreader, Jessica Fraser, for your suggestions. And thanks to my other proofreader, Tammy Payne, for picking up all those last minute typos.

As I've mentioned before, I adore my covers for this series. The typography has all been done by the very talented Daqri from Covers by Combs, and the image for Cold Sinful Revenge is Diogo from Wander Photography. He was instantly Jayden Wynter to me!

And thank you to you, reader, for enjoying my books. I wouldn't be able to do this without you.

Until next time!

Marissa

About the Author

Marissa Farrar has always been in love with being in love. But since she's been married for numerous years and has three young daughters, she's conducted her love affairs with multiple gorgeous men of the fictional persuasion.

The author of more than forty novels, she has been a full-time author for the last eight years. She predominantly writes paranormal romance and fantasy but has branched into contemporary fiction as well.

If you want to know more about Marissa, then please visit her website at www.marissa-farrar.com. You can also find her at her Facebook page, www.facebook.com/marissa.farrar.author or follow her on TikTok @marissafarrarwrites.

She loves to hear from readers and can be emailed at marissafarrar@hotmail.co.uk. To stay updated on all new releases and sales, just sign up to her newsletter!

Other Dark Contemporary Books by the Author

The Bad Blood Trilogy
Shattered Hearts
Broken Minds
Tattered Souls

The Monster Trilogy:
Defaced
Denied
Delivered

Dark Codes: A Reverse Harem Series
Hacking Darkness
Unraveling Darkness
Decoding Darkness
Merging Darkness

For Him Trilogy
Raised for Him
Unbound for Him
Damaged for Him

Standalone Novels:
No Second Chances
Cut Too Deep
Survivor
Dirty Shots